WIFE

Reasonably attractive wife wanted for handsome, wealthy rancher.

Must be able to marry immediately, cook a hearty meal and handle an exasperating man.

No experience necessary— at your own risk.

Please apply in person to Cleo Lawrence, c/o Gallagher Ranch, Oklahoma.

Please address questions and book requests to: Silhouette Reader Service
U.S.: 3010 Walden Ave., P.O. Box 1325, Buffalo, NY 14269
Canadian: P.O. Box 609, Fort Erie, Ont. L2A 5X3

Hitched in Haste

WESTERN *Lovers*

DIXIE BROWNING

THE HAWK AND THE HONEY

Silhouette Books

Published by Silhouette Books

America's Publisher of Contemporary Romance

To a certain entomologist
out in the panhandle.
Thanks, Bill.

SILHOUETTE BOOKS
300 East 42nd St.,
New York, N.Y. 10017

ISBN 0-373-88510-5

THE HAWK AND THE HONEY

One

The letter had been lying buried under a pile of newspapers on the coffee table for three days. It resurfaced when Cleo slid her attaché case across the heap, and she reached for it with a groan that expressed guilt, weariness and frustration. Another deathbed message from Wint, and she'd forgotten all about it. Poor Wint. He deserved better than that from his only living relative, but if he didn't cry "wolf" in every other letter, she might be more inclined to take him seriously. Not that she hadn't a dozen legitimate reasons for not going out to visit him. It was thirteen hundred miles, for goodness' sake, and that was only one way. She might fly to Amarillo or Liberty and rent a car, but even then, it was an undertaking. She'd made the trip twice, both times with her parents. The last time had been almost seventeen years ago.

Unfolding the single page of lined paper, she reread the penciled words. "Thank you for the wool socks and the gloves. I can't hardly get gloves on over these poor crippled hands of mine no more, but I guess cold weather won't be worrying me much longer."

"Oh, hell!" Cleo stepped out of her pumps and unfastened the waistband of her gabardine skirt. With one hand, she yanked the pins from her light brown, shoulder-length hair and allowed its freedom. "Just what I need—a load of guilt!"

She read on. Wint wouldn't *dream* of asking her to come all that way just to see her old great-uncle one last time, even though she *was* his own dead brother's granddaughter and he hadn't seen her since she was a little girl. Just send him a picture of her so that he could gaze on her sweet face one last time before his old eyes closed in blessed peace.

"Blessed peace, my foot, you wily old reprobate." Cleo grinned in spite of herself. They'd corresponded regularly since her last visit to the Oklahoma panhandle when she was fifteen. There'd been an instant affinity between the girl and the old man, for all their differences in age and background. He'd been vigorous enough then—a blacksmith on the cattle ranch where he still lived. Most of his letters now were about his bees and his chickens and what went on up at the main house, and at least once a year he hinted none too subtly at his imminent demise. It had been imminent now for a dozen or more years. Maybe if she kept putting off a visit, he'd live forever. He was stubborn enough to do just that.

Dropping the letter, Cleo stood up and stretched. The past few weeks, since the announcement of the move, had been killers. If the next few were as bad, then her decision was a foregone conclusion; she'd give notice. Six years of putting up with Rand Smith was all any woman should have to take. Between his total lack of qualifications for the job he held and his constant sniping, she was almost ready to throw in the towel.

"Every time I hire a woman over a man," she had told Reba McGuire from purchasing that morning, "I have to listen to half a dozen cracks about women's lib and affirmative action. Of course, if I hire a marginally qualified man over a highly qualified woman, that's just lovely, but let me go the other way and you'd think I was about to bring civilization to a screeching halt."

"So what else is new?" Reba had sympathized. "If it's any consolation, righteous indignation does marvelous things for your looks. Whoever said gray eyes were serene hasn't seen yours, and your complexion's just glowing."

"Dammit, he's going to stay on here until he's a hundred and one just to keep me from moving up," Cleo had grumbled, running her fingers through a once-neat fringe of bangs. "As if I hadn't already been doing his job for the past three years."

Stepping out of her skirt, she hung it up and unbuttoned her gray silk blouse. She had half promised to meet Reba and Debbie for a movie, but the lure of a long, hot soak and the new book on weaving she'd picked up on the way home won out. The movie was a love story, anyway, and she was in no mood for fairy tales.

Over baked potato and salad, she read Wint Lawrence's letter again. Spending a week out in the Oklahoma panhandle had been a memorable experience all those years ago. Even her parents' tight-lipped silences had been bearable. They'd grown noticeably more tight-lipped when her mother had discovered that they were to stay in Wint's mobile home near the back entrance to the vast Gallagher ranch. Her mother had fully expected to be invited to stay in the main house, but as Wint had explained, Dave Gallagher ran an all-male establishment, and he wasn't geared for female guests. Not that it had bothered Cleo. It hadn't even occurred to her that Mr. Gallagher might entertain the relatives of one of his employees, and she'd been thrilled at the novelty of the mobile home. It had been a wonderful vacation. She'd hung on to the warm memory of it all through the difficult years that followed—the divorce of her parents, the death of her father and her mother's remarriage.

What she wouldn't give for a dose of that carefree life right now—a week of riding and roaming, eating chili, barbecued beef and raw onions, seeing nothing but glorious empty space dotted with cattle, windmills and pumperjacks. It would be a relief from her doll-size apartment, which was threatening to go condo, from her nine-to-five job, which always seemed to stretch from eight to seven, from Rand Smith's perpetual disapproval, and most of all, from the nagging question of whether or to not to pull up stakes and move with the plant.

It was precisely nine-fifteen the following morning when Cleo thrust out her jaw and rapped on the door of the personnel director of Rand Knitting Mill. There had been a time when she'd fully expected to be sitting behind that big, genuine-walnut desk herself instead of behind a mountain of forms, applications, memos and government regulations at a smaller, wood-grained plastic one. Rand was sixty-one and had been with the company for thirty-seven years. He had the magic numbers; why wouldn't he retire and give her a chance? She was doing his job for him while he wore the title, drew the salary and took three-hour lunches, half-day golf dates and two or three so-called business trips a month. But his mother had been a Rand, and in this neck of the woods, that was carte blanche.

Exactly thirty minutes later, Cleo closed the door softly behind her and leaned against it. Blowing the fringe of brown hair from her forehead, she closed her eyes momentarily and wondered what on earth had gotten into her. Ultimatums weren't her style. But neither was martyrdom. Twice that year she had postponed her annual vacation for Rand's convenience. It was already November. At that rate, she'd wind up forfeiting the whole thing. Company policy forbade the carrying over of vacations.

A slow smile spread over her face as she mentally scanned the past half hour. In spite of Rand's protests and veiled threats, she hadn't backed down an inch on a single point. Five days from that day, she'd begin her three-week vacation, plus the additional two-day Thanksgiving holiday—she'd had to argue that point. He'd tried to run them concurrently.

The smile faded. At the end of that time, she'd have to decide one way or another about the move. The plant was shutting down its Burlington operation and moving to South Carolina, and Cleo had been among those offered the option of transferring. She'd been putting off making the decision, but she couldn't postpone it forever. By the time she came back, her decision would be due.

Stretching to ease the accumulated stiffness after two days on the road, Cleo looked over the selection of lunch possibilities at an exit just east of Oklahoma and decided on Lorena's Lounge and Country Kitchen. It was a break from the familiar franchise places, and she needed a break. In fact, it occurred to her that she'd been needing a vacation of some sort for ages. Rand had been pushing her to the point where she was almost ready to quit. Knowing it was only because he couldn't bear to retire and have his two-toned wing tips filled by a woman didn't help matters, either. If she stayed on, she'd be in for more of the same. She'd made some good friends in Burlington in the years that she'd been working there, and not all of them would be making the move with the plant. On the other hand, good jobs in her line weren't all that easy to come by these days.

Swinging back on I-40, Cleo concentrated on the increasing traffic. Only two days on the road and she'd already had enough of motels and fast-food chains. Lorena's Lounge had been a lucky find, and barring trouble, she'd be bedding down that night in Wint's mobile home instead of in another motel.

If she'd known how satisfying it was to turn on to I-40 back home in Carolina and follow it all the way to Oklahoma City, she might have done it sooner. The last trip had seemed unending, but that had been due to her mother's complaints and her father's hostile silences. Driving the distance alone was surprisingly pleasant. Maybe she'd quit her job as assistant personnel director and learn to drive an eighteen wheeler.

As she headed west from Woodward, the sun backlighted mile after mile of wild grasses, mingling the subtle hues and cast-

ing into relief the graceful, twisted shapes of
swamp willows along the numerous dry
creek beds. How could she have forgotten
the unbelievable colors and textures of this
high, empty land? Elm trees, shaped by the
summer's prevailing winds, bent over the
narrow highway. Pumperjacks were every-
where then, and the windmills that dotted
the landscape—she'd almost forgotten
those. Some were still in use to water stock;
others were weeded over as newer methods
supplanted the old.

Some three hours later, noting the state
road Wint had told her to watch for, Cleo
slowed down. There was practically no traffic, and she took the time to admire the
newly greening acres of winter wheat and the
intervening fallow fields.

The entrance was new, leading off from a
state road that hadn't even been paved when
she was last there. Instead of the old wooden
arch announcing the Gallagher ranch, there
was a new gate. An all metal, no-nonsense
affair, it opened on to a well-maintained
private road that ran straight as an arrow for
perhaps a mile and then disappeared over the
hill. And there, not a quarter of a mile from

the entrance to all this lush, oil-well-dotted
ranch land, was Wint's mobile home, seventeen years older, seventeen times more
rundown, surrounded by a motley collection of assorted fences that separated a goat
from a scruffy flock of chickens. Those pe-
culiar-looking white boxes plopped down in
a drunken row must be the bee gums he had
written her about. A television antenna
leaned dispiritedly atop a tall mast, and one
faded flannel shirt waved stiffly from the
short stretch of clothesline.

"Oh, Uncle Wint," Cleo groaned,
switching off the engine to lean her head
back for a moment. Here she'd been griping
about living in a tiny one-bedroom apartment and being too tired to cook more than
once or twice a week, and her only relative
was living all alone out there, in the back of
beyond, in what could only be described as
squalor. She felt incredibly mean.

"Things has changed considerable,"
Winston Lawrence affirmed, nodding his
head. They were seated at the small red-
topped table over bowls of chili, and Cleo
was finding it almost impossible to keep her
eyes from the dense crop of blue-black hair

that topped his weathered features. Wint must have been well over seventy. He'd been graying seventeen years before.

"When old Dave died, the boy come home to run things. College educated, he is. Weren't enough to go to Stillwater. No-siree bob, he had to go on to one of them fancy eastern schools."

"Look who's sneering at *eastern*," Cleo teased, knowing full well her great-uncle had been born in North Carolina the same as she had.

"I been here in these hills going on sixty years now," he told her, spooning a heap of chopped raw onion into his second bowl of chili. "I'm more Sooner than Tarheel."

"The tar just shifted to your head, and I'm not sure it's all on the outside, either."

The old man grinned, revealing a perfect set of teeth that were all his own—bought and paid for, as he proudly claimed. "Makes me look younger, don't it? How d'ye like it? The way that boy's turning things upside down around here, I thought I'd better spruce up a mite."

"Has he said anything to you?" Cleo asked, twisting to place her bowl and mug in the sink. One thing about staying in a two-bedroom trailer—her own tiny apartment was going to seem spacious by comparison.

"Not directly, but I can see which way the wind's blowing. First thing he done was to turn the danged place around—put the front round where the back used to be as soon as the county paved the road. I reckon them fancy friends of his'n complained o' getting dusty when they drove in the old way."

Cleo washed the few dishes while Wint rambled on about the changes. Her mind was more concerned with the problem confronting her than with the Gallagher boy's fastidious friends. Evidently, Gallagher, Junior, wasn't cut from the same bolt of cloth as his father had been. Second-generation money could be tricky to handle. Look at Rand Smith, for instance. His father had quit school in the seventh grade, made a mint in fortified wines, married into textile money and produced a son who had to prove his worth by putting down anyone with any degree of ability, especially if that person happened to be a woman.

"Next thing he done was to change over from a cow-calf operation to stocker," Wint rambled. Cleo twisted the dishcloth ruthlessly and resolved to put Rand Smith out of her mind. "Figgered he knew better than his daddy. Sold off ever' one o' them pure-bred Angus."

Cleo knew less than nothing about ranching operations, but she gathered from her great-uncle's tone of voice that the "boy" was only after a fast buck. How sad to fall heir to all these beautiful acres and be unable to see beyond the immediate gains.

"Then he put in all this fancy irrigation instead of the old windmills—got enough pipeline to reach plum to Arkansas." The old man grumbled. "But up to the main house, he ran smack dab into Nollie. Met his match there, he has. Old Nollie, he won't put up with no foolishness. He's looked after Gallagher's since Noah's ark ran aground, and ain't nobody going to tell him how to run that house. Stubborn old coot; he's too cussed mean to give up."

The following afternoon Cleo took the liberty of driving around the ranch. She'd forgotten most of it, remembering only the novelty of living in a trailer and the vast openness of the country. According to Wint, the ranch was some twenty-eight sections, which meant it was almost eighteen thousand acres. She tried to visualize the size and failed. Size was unimportant, anyway. It was the colors and textures that appealed to her. In the back of her mind, an idea began simmering, and she was glad she'd brought along a small loom and enough yarn to play with. She'd taken a course in weaving a couple of years ago, although she hadn't done much with it. There never seemed to be enough time to do more than read a few articles and admire what others had done.

Topping the next hill, she was confronted by the main house, a two-story white frame building that was perfectly square and completely unadorned by anything more decorative than a lightning rod. With its uncompromising lines and its steeply pitched, four-sided roof, it was hardly the home she'd have imagined for a man who owned all this. Behind the house, a line of clothes flapped stiffly in the ever-present wind. Evidently, old Nollie disdained the use of a drier. She could picture him tossing the family wash into an iron pot and boiling it down with a chunk of homemade lye soap.

Backing over a cattle guard, she turned around and headed back to the trailer.

By the third day, Cleo had managed to give the trailer a thorough turnout without doing too much damage to Wint's ego. The sheets in her room, obviously brand-new, with the label still intact, had stood out pathetically against the clutter of years of Wint's slapdash housekeeping. He had modestly admitted to making a special trip into Guymon to purchase the yellow linens and a set of lurid pink towels just for her, and she was touched.

In spite of Wint's claim that his bees were as gentle as butterflies, Cleo refused to go near the boxes. She did enjoy the chickens, however. The eight colorful bantam roosters noisily scrabbled over every blade of grass, and Cleo loved tossing in handfuls of scratch feed and watching the protocol. It was a little like the jockeying for position that went on in higher management back at work.

Dressed in jeans and one of Wint's old wool-lined denim jackets, she was trying to lure a certain rooster to eat from her hand when she heard a truck turn into what passed for a front yard. She'd met two of the hands since she'd been there and was relieved to find that her uncle didn't lack for companionship. It was probably another one, and she wasn't particularly anxious to be shown off at the moment. Wint's pride in her was heartwarming, but dressed as she was, with her light brown hair standing on end from this devilish wind, she wasn't anything to brag about. She'd spent the morning wandering on foot, looking for the arrowheads she had childishly expected to litter the ground and collecting an assortment of lovely dried grasses and seed heads.

The kitchen window was slightly open because the small trailer overheated so quickly, and the voices inside came through clearly to mingle with the contented murmurings of the chickens.

"Been here three days a'ready. Likes the place—took to it when she was a young'un, just like I told you."

They were talking about her. Cleo tossed out the last of the corn and brushed off her hands before raking her fingers through her shoulder-length hair. Her usual standards of grooming were a thing of the past—not that

Wint's friends, Rado and Josie, seemed to notice. They'd stood, hats in hand, and beamed at her silently while she'd tried to draw them into a conversation.

"Good breedin' stock, too," Wint was saying. She was off the hook; they'd gone on to discuss cattle. "A mite long in the tooth, but then you want one with some age onto 'er. Them flighty young things that come traipsin' out here from the city ain't gonna do you no good. No-siree bob, you need a woman who can pull her weight. Now this gal of mine, she's smart as a whip—college educated like you are, but she's a doer, too. Why she hadn't no more than set foot in here than she started in on this place of mine. Lookee here! See the shine on them winders?"

There was a baritone rumble, and Cleo moved closer to the back of the trailer, unashamedly eavesdropping. If her uncle thought for one minute she was going to hire on as old Nollie's replacement, he was in for a disappointment.

"She's good stock. I'll fetch her in here now'n a minute, and you just take a look at

them hips. She'll breed you up a passel
o'boys before you know it, and you can jest
set back and—"

Cleo didn't wait to hear more. That
sneaking, conniving old con artist was trying to marry her off to some damned cowboy! So that was why he'd practically
blackmailed her into coming all the way out
here to see him *one last time.* She'd "one last
time" him!

Not even pausing to cool the flame that
temper always brought to her cheeks, Cleo
shoved open the back door and presented
herself, hands on her well-advertised hips
and gray eyes flinty. "Wint, if you think for
one..." Her voice trailed off as she got a
good look at the man her uncle was proposing to auction her off to. He stood tall
enough in his dusty western boots to graze
the ceiling, and his shoulders could have
easily carried a bale of hay apiece. His deep-
set eyes appeared colorless at first, but they
didn't miss much in their leisurely tour of her
own lean five feet eight inches.

"Miss Lawrence, I'm Roane Gallagher,"
the man said quietly. It was a watchful qui-

etness, as if he suspected she was going to blow and he wanted to be warned in time to duck.

"How do you do." It was no question. She didn't give a damn how he did, and he knew it. Tight-lipped, she cast a speaking look at her uncle and then confronted Roane Gallagher again. In spite of a hairline that had eroded beyond the tumbled black widow's peak, he was strikingly attractive, his features strong and just irregular enough to be interesting. If this was the "boy" who was reshaping the Gallagher empire, she couldn't see him being manipulated by a bad-tempered old cook—or a cunning, arthritic ex-blacksmith, either.

"I hope you weren't offended by my uncle's idea of a joke, Mr. Gallagher. Wint has a great sense of humor," she added sarcastically.

"Not at all, Miss Lawrence. In fact, I appreciate his concern for my well-being. Wint knows how much my place needs a woman's touch. He's obviously luckier in that respect than I am."

If that was her cue to offer to play house-keeper, he could forget it. She'd had the "woman's place" approach up to here!

Wint sidled up to her, his wizened stature no match for her militant stance. "Ah, now, Cleo, don't get your dander up! I just thought since you hadn't had no luck findin' yourself a man back East and Roane here needed a wife, I'd do the two of you a favor."

"I can't believe I'm hearing this," Cleo marveled. "Mr. Gallagher, you'll have to forgive my uncle. It's obvious that living alone with only a swarm of bees, a flock of chickens and a goat for company has warped his mind."

Roane grinned, making his long, angular face seem even more attractive. "Seems to me the only thing out of line is Wint's notion that you couldn't find a man for yourself. For my part, I'm beginning to think the idea has distinct possibilities."

Raking her long fingers through her gleaming, wind-tossed hair, Cleo stared at him. "Possibilities! You're as bad as he is! Look, if you're that hard up for a wife, why not just get a catalogue and order yourself one, but don't look at me. I'm permanently out of stock"

This was preposterous. Who'd believe Cleo Lawrence, assistant personnel director of Rand's, could be standing there in the middle of nowhere in a run-down trailer, fielding a proposal from an oil and cattle baron? In spite of her irritation, a reluctant smile began to curl the edges of her wide mouth. "Why do I have the feeling that any minute now you're going to peel back my lips and examine my teeth?"

An answering grin crinkled Roane Gallagher's strong features. "Speaking of teeth, it occurs to me that I've been remiss in my manners, Miss Lawrence. You've been here three days, and I haven't invited you up to the house for dinner."

Cleo's smile faltered briefly as she recalled how eagerly her mother would have snapped up such an invitation. As Wint's eager gaze moved back and forth between them, she said firmly, "Thanks, but it's not at all necessary. Uncle Wint and I are doing just fine on our own." It was a sure bet he didn't usually invite her uncle to dinner up on the hill. Why should he feel obligated to entertain the Lawrences now?

"Please—I can't offer you much in the way of gourmet fare, but I'd very much appreciate it if you and Wint would dine with me tonight. Maybe Nollie will try a little harder with company to please. I guess Wint's told you about Nollie. His cooking doesn't kill outright, but it can bore you to death. Good dinner companions help ease the pain."

What could she say? Somehow the tables had been cleverly turned, and she felt it would be churlish to refuse. Besides, from the gleam she had caught in Roane Gallagher's eyes—they were the palest brown she'd ever seen—she rather suspected that he was amused at Wint's outrageous tactics. It really was pretty funny now that she'd gotten over the initial shock of hearing her finer points brought out in such a manner.

Good *breeding* hips? She knew she wasn't a bean pole, but then she wasn't exactly matronly, either.

Bemused, she heard herself agreeing to six-thirty on the hill. Thank goodness she'd stuck a dress in her case—although if the Gallagher household was as bad as she'd been led to believe, maybe she'd better stick to pants. A skirt might affect old Nollie the way a red cape affected a bull.

Two

In the end, Cleo compromised on white silk pants and a jade velvet tunic. Entering the stark foyer with Wint, who was resplendent in western gear, she wished she'd worn something a little less opulent. The house was cold, colorless and totally uninviting.

"Sorry about all this," Roane apologized, gesturing vaguely to the unadorned, white wooden walls and the darkly varnished floor semicovered with an ugly rug that was too small for the space. He led them into a room that wasn't much better. There the same white painted walls prevailed, but this time they were accompanied by an assortment of graceless furniture that was as uncomfortable as it was unattractive. A pitiless light shone down from a wrought-iron overhead fixture, the only decent-looking thing in the room. Roane poured a drink for Wint and asked Cleo her preference.

"To tell you the truth, I'm inclined to forget how bad this place is until I see it as a background for someone like you," Roane said.

Cleo lifted a brow at the "someone like you." She preferred to think she was unique, but what difference did it make? She'd probably see nothing more of the man before she left, anyway. Her one and only brush with the Oklahoma oil and cattle aristocracy would be good for a laugh or two with Reba and Debbie, and then it would be filed and forgotten.

"Evidently, it doesn't bother you too much, or you'd do something about it." If that bordered on rudeness, chalk it up to the odd effect Roane had on her. His eyes had a disconcerting way of looking directly into hers and eliminating the usual constraint between strangers. She'd never experienced anything quite like it, and she wasn't certain she trusted it. Cleo was outgoing and friendly by nature, but not, as a rule, with men. There was always that thin shield of scar tissue that prevented her from allowing any man to get within striking distance.

Roane saw them seated and then eased his lean length into one of the heavy, black oak chairs. "In the year and a half since I came back home, I haven't had too much time to think about interior decoration. By the time I finish up for the day, food and sleep are about all I'm interested in."

Wint leaned forward, his twisted fingers cupped on bony knees clad in stiff new jeans. "Don't tell me them fillies I see parading past my place is county agents workin' overtime."

In spite of their relative positions, there was nothing at all condescending in Roane's grin as he scoffed, "Now come on, Wint. You didn't think I'd joined a monastery, did you? I left some pretty good friends back in Tulsa and Oklahoma City, and a man likes to keep in touch."

"Do a dang sight more'n touchin', I'd lay odds," Wint muttered, fingering the silver-tipped tie he wore with his flowered western-style shirt.

The summons to dinner came in the form of a rasping voice urging them to "come and git it." Roane nodded to the double door, allowing Wint to precede him as he placed a hand lightly on Cleo's back. His touch was completely impersonal, but for some strange reason, she stiffened instinctively. It was too much to hope that he hadn't noticed, but at least he was courteous enough to ignore it, except for one swift, quizzical glance.

"I always did like the feel of velvet," he murmured, ushering her into another of the square, stark rooms that seemed to abound in this square, stark house. "What color would you call that blouse of yours?"

"Green," she said flatly.

One corner of his mobile mouth twitched as he seated her at the scarred oval table. "I thought I recognized it."

The tureen was Spode, with one handle broken off. The ladle was blue enameled steel. Roane served, and Wint scowled suspiciously at the watery soup. When a dried-up raisin of a man sidled in bearing a platter of some unidentifiable substance, Wint snorted.

"What's this you're a-fixin' to pizen us with? Tick dip?"

The man in the filthy apron shifted his cigar to the other side of his toothless mouth and scowled back. "Ain't no self- respectin' tick'd come within a mile of you since you took to polishin' yer head with stove black."

Cautiously, Cleo tasted the soup. She looked up to find Roane's amused gaze on her, and he said in a low voice, "Do the best you can with it. It's probably nourishing."

It wasn't that it was bad; it was simply tasteless. She managed to get down almost a third of it before she gave up, but as Roane dished up the stringy, grayish meat and the assorted soggy vegetables that had been boiled with it, she felt the last of her appetite slip away.

"I wondered what they done with that old bull o' Ramos's that got tangled up in the wire and broke his leg," Wint grumbled as Nollie removed the soup plates. "He don't taste half bad for a ten-year-old, Nol."

The cook-housekeeper muttered something unintelligible around the stub of his unlit cigar and shouldered open the door to the kitchen. Cleo shoved her plate aside and looked helplessly at her host.

"I apologize, Cleo. Actually, the fare's a little better than usual tonight. Probably in your honor."

"Whut wuz them yeller thangs?" Wint inquired with suspect guilelessness. "Horse apples?"

"What on earth are horse apples?" Cleo asked.

"Osage oranges," Roane replied. "And no, I think these particular yellow things were rutabagas, but the less said about them, the better. Shall we adjourn to the living room for coffee?"

Wint stood and hitched the silver-buckled belt around his scrawny waist. "I'll jest set in the kitchen while Nollie boils the coffee up to see he don't leave the eggshells in when he settles the grounds." His expression was so outrageously coy that it was all Cleo could do to keep from laughing.

"Alone at last. What do you suppose he expects of us now?" Roane murmured as he ushered her back into the cheerless living room. He seated her on the uncompromising black leather sofa and took the other end, propping a booted foot on the edge of a scarred coffee table.

"I'm more interested in what to expect of Nollie's coffee," Cleo replied. "Does he really boil it with eggshells?"

"Only at breakfast," Roane told her gravely. His square, callused hands unwrapped a slender cigar efficiently, and he raised a querying brow before lighting it. "Other times, he just boils it until it's thick enough and then dribbles a little cold water down the edge of the pan to settle the grounds. It's not half bad once you get used to it."

"Heaven forbid," Cleo uttered fervently, thinking of her small electric grinder and the filter coffee maker at home. "Why do you put up with it? Can't you . . . retire him?"

Roane eased his position, and Cleo's eyes were drawn to the long muscular thighs covered with beige whipcord. The brown shirt he wore, for all its casual styling, was silk, and she was obscurely glad she'd worn the flattering jade and white outfit. Not that it mattered. One night—a few hours at most—and then she'd never see him again. He was incredibly attractive, though, she mused. Those weathered features, that M-shaped hairline, the work-honed fitness of his powerful body—it all added up to a type of ultramasculinity she had seldom, if ever, run across.

"The trouble is," Roane drawled, "when a man was practically born into a particular job and devotes his whole life to it, how the devil do you tell him that he's past it? Those two in there"—he nodded to the kitchen—"they've been here since before I was born. They helped build this place. How can I tell them they're no longer needed? Wint, at least, was forced to quit when his hands got so they couldn't do the work. He was a top-notch blacksmith and all-around hand, and he still pulls his weight around here with the bees."

Nollie shouldered his way in with a battered tray holding two mugs, a crusty sugar bowl and a pitcher of milk. He plopped them down on the coffee table with a suspicious look at Cleo. When he'd gone, she reached hesitantly for one of the steaming mugs. "He looked as if he thought I might ram a few spoons in my purse. Is he always this suspicious of visitors?"

Without answering, Roane poured milk in her mug, and she protested. "But I don't—"

"This time you'd better," he told her wryly. "Milk—"

"Lines the stomach," Cleo finished, and they both grinned spontaneously in shared amusement. There it was again, this strange feeling of intimacy, as if they had known each other for ages. "So why did he give me that peculiar look? Is he waiting to see the effect of his cooking? Is the coffee supposed to be a sort of antidote? Or maybe the coup de grace?"

"Jealous of his territory, probably. He's this way with most women. So's Wint, as a rule, but of course, in your case—"

"Don't remind me," she shuddered, tucking one foot up under her on the cushion. Somewhere along the line, the foot had slipped itself out of its sandal, and she was amazed at how comfortable she had become, considering the surroundings and the circumstances. "You were saying... about the bees?"

"Bees? As in birds and—" Roane shot her a quizzical look.

"As in Wint's bees," she reminded him swiftly, daring a sip of the thick beverage in her mug. It wasn't so bad, after all—an acquired taste, perhaps, like espresso or Turkish coffee.

"Oh. Wint's bees. Well, we grow several crops—wheat, small grain sorghum, alfalfa and the like. Crops have to be pollinated, and wild bees have a hard time these days, with the sprays and such. Wint manages to keep us in bees and honey, and that's a real service. He sells the extra honey through a market in Guymon, so it works out just fine. Now," he said, with a glinting grin, "about the other kind of bees—"

"Never mind. I studied birds and bees in junior high. Things haven't changed all that much since then."

The companionable silence between them lengthened as they finished their coffee. Roane stubbed out his cigar and turned to her, and Cleo lifted her chin as the first fine edge of wariness crept in. Instinctively, she went about setting out the keep-out signs she had used for the previous ten years. In that uncanny silent communication that had sprung up so unexpectedly between them, Roane acknowledged the barriers and leaned back against the corner of the sofa, his crossed arms informing her that he was no longer a threat to her security. Her gray eyes lightened perceptibly as she relaxed.

"So tell me. What do you do back in North Carolina, Cleo Lawrence?"

She could deal with words. Questions and answers were the tools she worked with every day, and she could usually manage to fence with them quite skillfully. "Do you want a title or a job description? The two aren't exactly the same."

"Both." His smile lifted a bit more on the left side than the right, calling her attention to the contrast between his chiseled upper lip and the fuller bottom one.

She yanked her attention away quite forcefully. "Assistant personnel director of a textile plant. We make nightgowns, ladies' pajamas and slips."

"Hmmm, that could be fascinating work. Tell me, do you make the satin and lace variety or the striped flannel?" His light brown eyes held a teasing light, but his arms remained crossed over his massive chest.

"Satin and lace, but I'm more concerned with our people than our product. I can have a catalogue sent out here if you're really interested. Some of your, ah—weekend visitors might enjoy it. Or are they really county agents?" she added innocently.

One dark brow lifted in amusement. "Surely you're not implying that all county agents sleep in striped flannel. Who knows, maybe I could get a higher protein rating for my alfalfa if I slipped someone a slip on the sly."

She grimaced at the terrible play on words. "I'll tell you what—when I mail you the catalogue, I'll *slip* in a collection of underwear jokes. They run through the mill like ladders in hosiery."

"If you think those are bad, wait until you taste a sample of what passes for ranch humor." He grinned, and Cleo replied that Wint had already initiated her.

"Between the pair of them, Wint and Nol, they've heard 'em all. In fact, I expect they've invented their share." Roane extended his long legs across the table and crossed his booted ankles, favoring her with a look of relaxed interest. "Wint told me once that he came from a long line of coast guardsmen. How'd he wind up out here blacksmithing?"

"I'm not sure. Ask him three times and you get three different answers. His brother, my grandfather, was a chief warrant officer, and Daddy was a group commander. I gather Wint didn't take well to obeying orders, either his family's or anyone else's. Or maybe he was just one of those little boys who grow up wanting to be cowboys." She studied him candidly. "Did you?"

"Can't say I ever gave it much thought." His gaze ranged over her face as if gauging the depth of her interest. "Dave—my father, that is—expected me to carry on what he had started. It's a lot different these days than it was when cattle were moved on the hoof and a man had to spend weeks, even months, in the saddle." His features took on a pensive look for a moment.

Then, on a different note, he said, "Personnel work, hmm? Maybe you can understand my problem with Nollie. A tractor, I could trade in. A bull could be put out to pasture, but how does a man deal with something like this?"

"I suppose each case is different. Sometimes it just seems to fall together so that everyone's happy, but sometimes..." She eyed him speculatively. "Wint seemed to think all you had to do was bring home a bride and things would get sorted out."

"Is that an offer?" He shot her a mildly salacious look.

"No way. I just thought since I was out here in the wild and woolly West, I'd take the bull by the horns, so to speak."

"Too bad. The idea's starting to grow on me."

"Try a fungicide," Cleo offered dryly, and his laughter rang out in the chilly room.

"Seriously, Wint is right. About the only way I'm going to get Nol pried loose from this place is to bring home a wife, and I couldn't guarantee even that would do the trick."

"How did things get to this state?"

The laughter flickered in his eyes again as he said, "That old man's been running my life since I was in short pants. He cleaned me up after my first plug of chewing tobacco, and he was the one who taught me how to drink and when to quit. You don't think he has any respect for me now, do you?''

At his plaintive tone, Cleo allowed her amusement full play. It was literally impossible to think of Roane Gallagher as anything but the magnificently assured creature he now was. ''I can see that you might have a tiny problem there,'' she ventured. ''So now you need a skirt to hide behind. Surely you must know lots of suitable candidates. What about those visitors Wint was talking about, the ones who followed you home from the city?'' With unselfconscious curiosity, she added, ''What were you doing in the city, anyway? Herding mechanical bulls?''

''Running a Christmas tree outfit.''

''You're kidding! Growing them or trimming them?'' Her foot had gone to sleep, and she lowered it to the floor and wriggled her toes.

''Gas-well equipment—it's called Christmas trees. I was part owner of a plant outside Tulsa.''

''Do you miss it? City life, I mean?''

Studying the tip of his gleaming, well-worn boot, Roane appeared to consider his answer. "No, I don't think I do. Not that it would make any difference, since I'm here for keeps." He lapsed into a silence that lasted for several minutes, and oddly enough, Cleo was perfectly comfortable in the bleak surroundings. Roane's powerful personality more than made up for the shortcomings of his home.

After a while, he began speaking again, the softness of his deep drawl almost disguising the underlying granite. "I didn't exactly see eye to eye with Dave—my father. Too much alike, I guess. We were both too headstrong to work well together, but I could never sell the ranch. It was always understood between us that I'd take over if he needed me. Unfortunately, his first heart attack was also his last, so the load hit my back pretty unexpectedly. By the time I could wind up my affairs in Tulsa, things here had already started getting slack, but we're back on course now."

Cleo tried to remember Dave Gallagher from the one time she'd seen him. Her only impression was of a man built like an oak tree and every bit as hard and unyielding. His son was essentially the same, but there was an underlying element of something else, something that made him more dangerous than his father could ever have been. Dangerous, at least, where women were concerned. What had his mother been like? She'd never heard a word about a Mrs. Gallagher. Maybe there'd never been one. Maybe Roane had sprouted from an acorn. At the idea, a smile softened her lips.

"What's so funny?"

"Oak—acorn," she said without thinking, and then she could have kicked herself for assuming that he'd understand. Just because their thoughts seemed to have run together a few times—it was probably all her imagination, anyway. "I was wondering if you'd sprouted from an acorn," she blurted, muddling matters even more. "I just meant that Dave reminded me of a tree when I was young." So much for poise and savoir-faire.

"Yeah—Dave was an oak, all right. He swore I had a mother, but you can't prove it by me. Maybe you'd care to check me over for blight or tent worms?" He unfolded his arms and extended them along the top of the sofa.

"I'm sorry, Roane. I didn't mean to get personal. It's really none of my business. I guess I'm just too used to asking snoopy questions."

"No problem. My mother died before I was old enough to remember her, and Dave never talked about her. I expect that was when things started drying up here at home. Nollie stepped in to take over temporarily, and he's been here ever since. At this point, I don't know quite what to do about it."

"Maybe Wint's solution has some merit, after all. Oh, not me," she hastened to add when she caught his quick gleam of interest. "I'm not in the running, but surely you have someone in mind. You said yourself that you had a lot of good friends back in Tulsa and Oklahoma City. Why not pick out one of the more domesticated ones and pop the question?"

"I'm not sure I know how to tell the domesticated ones from the wild variety. Frankly, that hasn't been a part of my criteria up till now."

"Hmmm, I'll bet it hasn't," Cleo muttered in a low voice, then added, "Maybe you'd do better to look around closer to home."

Roane allowed his eyes to range over her with exaggerated interest, and Cleo shook her head warningly. She couldn't prevent the sparkle of amusement from dancing in her eyes, however, and at his answering grin, she burst into laughter. When they both managed to sober up, she said with mock severity, "What you need is an executive housekeeper, a tactful sort who can ease Nollie into semiretirement and then organize the household so that he'll still have his pride, plus a few responsibilities."

Roane flexed the arm that was resting on the back of the sofa as he stared thoughtfully at the toe of his boot. "That's a pretty tall order. Any woman who could handle Nollie could also run the United Nations and manage a baseball team in her spare time."

"Probably," Cleo agreed easily, and then grinned as he caught a handful of her hair and gave it a tug. "What you need is a little homebody, someone who's content just to run you, your ranch and all your employees. Better be sure she has a hobby, though. Otherwise, she might get bored with all the time on her hands.''

Roane's wicked smile promised retaliation, and Cleo felt a small rush of excitement along her spine.

''Unless I've been sadly misinformed,'' he observed, ''there's something more to this business of wifing than just keeping house. Maybe I could suggest a hobby for her, something we could both enjoy.''

''Both of you, huh?'' Cleo frowned and studied the ornate ceiling fixture. ''That narrows the field down considerably. A woman who can run a spread this size *and* play a good game of checkers.''

''Actually the hobby I had in mind was more along these lines.'' The hand on her shoulder tugged her off balance, and before she could right herself, his other arm turned her so that she was sprawled across his chest.

''Roane, don't be ridiculous.'' Cleo giggled, trying to maintain her dignity under impossible circumstances. One sandal was dangling from a toe, and it fell noisily to the floor, which didn't help matters much. Fumbling to right herself, her hand pushed against his stomach, encountering the heavily embossed silver buckle with the jasper cabochon. In jerking her hand back, she lost her precarious balance and fell back across his lap.

"Now come on, honey. You don't want to disappoint Wint and Nollie, do you? Ten to one they're behind the kitchen door laying odds on how fast I can get you into my bed."

"Roane, that's—will you stop that?" He was combing slowly through her hair, skeining the leaf-brown filaments through work-hardened fingers. His knuckles grazed her sensitive nape, and she caught her breath. This was utterly absurd. In spite of everything, she'd only met the man a few hours ago, and besides, she was too old to go in for wrestling on the sofa.

"You don't believe me?" he asked provocatively. "Cleo, honey, those two would bet on how many times a fly will rub its hind legs together between two lumps of sugar. We both know why Wint got you out here, so why pretend to be so surprised?"

It wasn't surprise, or even anger, that was elevating her pulses at the moment. She'd like to think it was the exercise, but she was in better physical shape than that. "Roane, I don't give a damn who bets on what. This game has gone far enough!"

His arm held her against him with deceptive ease, and she couldn't do a thing except flap her arms and kick out, both of which made her feel even more foolish. "Is this the technique you use bulldogging steers?" she jeered.

"Yes, ma'am. As a rule, it works pretty well with the heifers, too. Maybe you'd be so kind as to point out what I'm doing wrong." One of his hands came up under her hair to cup the back of her head in his capable palm. "Is this better?" he asked with mock gravity. "I can see right off where it might have its advantages." His face hovered only inches above hers, and she scowled up at him, seeing the way the lines rayed out at the corners of his eyes and flared down from his long, slightly crooked nose. He smiled lazily at her, and she took grim pleasure in noticing the chipped corner on one of his strong white teeth—as if such a flaw were an indication of weakness.

"Roane, if you're waiting for me to cry uncle, then consider it done. But if I really *do* and Wint comes barging in here, we're both going to look pretty silly."

"Yes, ma'am. I reckon you're right," he agreed with suspicious meekness. "By now, he'll expect us to be busy placing an order for our first son."

It was hopeless. Cleo closed her eyes in despair and uttered a mild oath. She could feel Roane's heart beneath her, the beat scarcely accelerated at all. His breath was warm and fragrant on her face, and she waited for the inevitable. When it did come, she opened one eye and then the other, and then she glared at him.

He was laughing at her! "Damn you, Roane Gallagher. Let me up. If I'd known I had to wrestle you for my dinner, I'd have stayed home and eaten Wint's red beans and onions again!"

"Sounds good. Invite me over."

"Wint can pay back your dubious hospitality after I've gone back home," she muttered, smoothing the jade velvet top after her impromptu wrestling match. She felt like an idiot. Thirty-two years old and here she was squirming around on the parlor sofa like a high school cheerleader with the star quarterback.

"I thought it was all settled that you wouldn't be going back home again."

"You thought what?" She stared at him, her mouth slightly open, and he leaned back and crossed those oak-limb arms over his chest again.

"You mean you're not going to marry me and take over my household? I thought that was what all this talk had been about." His expression was as innocent as any man of his age and experience could manage, she supposed.

The corners of her mouth quivered, and she forced them to be still, but there was little she could do about the light that danced in her gray eyes. "It breaks my heart to decline such a romantic offer, but I do have an alternative solution for you," she said sweetly.

Somewhere in the house, a door creaked, and she savored the thought that those two old reprobates were listening in. "A set of china. Choppers—false teeth," she elaborated at Roane's mystified look. "You see, the reason Nollie boils everything to death is because of his teeth—or lack of them. He'd starve on crunchy salads and corn on the cob. Just look at Wint, though. He eats anything he wants, and with those new teeth and his navy blue hair, he doesn't look a day over ninety-seven, either.''

The creak was louder this time, and with it came a muffled explosion of some sort. The door burst open, and Wint stalked in, glaring at her. "Aw right, we're goin' home! I don't know whut your mama taught you, girl, but it shore weren't manners!" He turned his pink-rimmed eyes at Roane and began apologizing for her. "An' to think I brang her out here for you to marry. I'm shore sorry, boy. That billy goat o' mine'd turn up his nose at a female who ain't got no more manners than to talk about her own flesh and blood thataway.''

Roane watched them through the window as they left. Wint's arthritis was bothering him again, but he'd chop off a fist before admitting it. What made old men so damned proud? Nollie, who didn't know when to give in, and that poor old devil with his dyed hair and his Corningware teeth. His own father had been something like that, come to think of it. Too stubborn to see that times were changing. He'd dug in and weathered so many hard times that he could never relax sufficiently to enjoy the good ones.

He watched the brief wrangle beside Cleo's car. Was she insisting on driving or insisting that he do it? Pride was a devilish thing at any age, and it seemed that the older a man got, the worse it was.

Wint took the wheel, and Roane thought he caught a glimmer of a smile on Cleo's face as she slid into the passenger seat. She was a hell of a woman. He wished he'd been there when she'd come out the last time. She'd have been just a girl then—long, lean, spirited, like that sorrel mare he'd been trying to break in his spare time. Something—a man, probably—had come close to breaking Cleo at some time in her past, he'd be willing to bet. It was there in the way she tilted that stubborn jaw of hers, in her eyes when she'd backed off from him. So close, they said, no closer. He could read the message loud and clear.

As the car left the lighted main yard for the darkness beyond, Roane moved away from the curtainless window. Funny, the old place hadn't seemed to bother her, for all it was as uninviting as a house could be. Lord knows he was aware of the shortcomings. He'd had a few friends out to visit since he'd come home. Marsha had been vocal enough from the time she'd set foot in there, and the others hadn't been much better. This one, though, had glanced around, shrugged as if it didn't really matter all that much and then forgotten about it.

She was a comfortable woman. He'd liked her looks when he'd first set eyes on her in Wint's trailer, mad as a hornet, her gray eyes shooting fire and her hair looking like loose-stacked hay. But she'd seen the funny side soon enough. She was good company. She was also good-looking, but it was her sense of the ridiculous that appealed to him. She could be a damned sight plainer, and he'd still enjoy her company.

Roane's footsteps echoed on the gritty floors. Nollie had already cleaned up and turned in, and the old house sounded hollow. It was too big, too empty. Back when he'd been growing up there, his father had seemed to take up the space of three ordinary men. Nollie had been a weathered, cantankerous runt all his life, but he'd run things well enough. There'd been a couple of boys to help out once, but they'd long since gotten fed up and moved on. It had always been a male stronghold. He was just now coming to realize how bleak and comfortless such a household was.

Still, it was only in the past few years that the food had gotten so bad. Maybe Cleo was right, and teeth were the answer. He grinned, picturing Wint's expression when he'd come charging into the room. She'd paid him back for the stunt he'd pulled that morning, all right.

Those two had more in common than they knew, he suspected—a strain of pure cussedness that would get them through the rough times. His dad had had it—hell, he probably had it himself. He hoped so. It was the same strain that had gotten Sooners through a lot of years of bust and boom. Back East, where Cleo came from, they were looking back on some four hundred years of history, but over eighty years ago, Oklahoma hadn't even been a state.

Funny how ideas could change. In Tulsa, he'd driven around in a forty-thousand-dollar car and eaten in the finest restaurants with some of the most beautiful women anywhere. Now he drove a pickup truck and ate poorly seasoned boiled beef and soggy vegetables with an eccentric old retired blacksmith and his outspoken great-niece.

And he'd laughed more that night than he had in ages. Lately, he'd been too busy, too preoccupied to laugh.

Cleo was different, all right. She was totally different from the sort of women he usually associated with. For one thing, there was nothing at all superficial about her. She hadn't winced when he'd propped his feet on the coffee table; she hadn't subjected him to the usual subtle—or sometimes not so subtle—questions about what he was worth. And she hadn't simpered her way through dinner trying to pretend she wasn't going to wind up in his bed.

His thoughts veered off on an interesting tangent. She'd be good in bed. There was a basic honesty about her that was refreshing, and come to think of it, he'd never slept with a woman who laughed so readily. Might be worth exploring....

Three

"Surely a man like Roane won't have any trouble finding himself a wife," Cleo observed at breakfast. She'd cooked buckwheat cakes that morning, and Wint had stacked half a dozen plate-sized ones and was busy drowning them with butter and honey.

"If he lived in Tulsa or Oklahoma City, it'd be a different thing. Trouble is, he got hisself a taste for big-city women, the kind that has to have French restaurants and toe

dancin' and pretty frocks and all that foo-
ferall.''

"I know plenty of women who like French
cooking and ballet and dress like models
who'd jump at a chance to marry a man like
Roane, and not just because of his money,
either.''

Wint grinned and snaked another slice of
bacon from the platter. "Thought you'd
taken a shine to him. You could go farther
and do worse, girl. No point in working out
the rest of your days in a noisy, dirty old mill
when you can live out here and breathe
God's good air.''

Thinking of the light, bright airiness of
the employees' lounge and the gleaming
plant cafeteria that boasted some of the best
food in town, Cleo smiled. "It's not exactly
a sweat shop, Uncle Wint, but even if it
were, I'd be going back. I'm not in the market for a husband. I'm sorry if you're disappointed, but after all, we can still keep in
touch. You might even come East for a
visit—I'd love to have you." Although it
might be South Carolina instead of North,
and who knows what sort of an apartment
she could find. She hated the idea of apart-

ment hunting again after all these years. In the newer ones her friends lived in, the walls were thinner, the rooms even smaller and the rent higher.

"But if you're all that concerned over Roane's plight," she said, seeing the downcast look on Wint's face, "I could invite a couple of friends out and try my hand at matchmaking." The joking offer came right off the top of her head, but she continued thoughtfully. "Actually, I ought to be pretty good at it—I've spent years matching up people and jobs. Why not people and people?"

Reba and Debbie would have a ball out there. One of the last things Debbie had said was "Bring me a souvenir from Oklahoma—how about an oillionaire?" Reba had stated her preference for a rodeo star, but both of them would be bowled over by Roane Gallagher, who was certainly the one and possibly the other.

"Yeah, an' the first thing one o' them fancy women'd do is to throw me plum off'n the place. I seen 'em turnin' up their noses when they ride by. They think a man that lives by hisself in a trailer and raises chickens and bees is one part crazy and three parts fool."

"If they turn up their noises, it's probably because of your goat," Cleo murmured dryly, scraping the plates and sliding them into the minuscule sink.

"Billy's a pet. A man's got a right to keep a pet, ain't he?"

"Billy's a stinking, rotten-tempered old he-goat who's either too lazy or too stupid to butt his way out of that pen, but I sure would love to have a handful of his hair to use in my weaving." She'd gazed longingly at the cantankerous old thing more than once, wondering how she could separate him from a hank of the long, silky white wisps that edged his brindle back.

Wint chuckled. "Jest help yourself, girlie. Ol' Billy'd be more'n willin' to oblige you if you ask him politely."

Later, tucking an apple into her knapsack with her sketching things, Cleo let herself out the back door. She studied the goat, who stared unblinkingly back at her. The aroma was bad enough, but it was the expression in those beady eyes that convinced her she'd do better to forget it. She'd hate to have to drive

thirteen hundred miles home sitting on a
donut cushion.

After a day spent exploring and sketching
and watching the gracefully soaring hawks
that hunted the countryside, Cleo wandered
back to the trailer. The sun threw a halo over
each billowy clump of dried grass and silhouetted the balls of tumbleweed that lined
the fences.

She felt good. She had a notebook filled
with ideas to transpose into fiber, and more
than once as she lay stretched out on a sunny
slope of unused pasture, inhaling the sweet
herbal scent and watching lazy-dumpling
clouds drift overhead, she'd smiled, remembering the previous night's dinner date. It
was surely one of the strangest she'd ever
had, and Roane, whether or not she wanted
to admit it, was one of the most attractive
men she'd ever met.

It wasn't only his looks, although Lord
knows they were spectacular enough in a
rugged, mature sort of way. It was his whole
attitude, his bearing, the fact that he could
move from a luxurious urban setting to one
of relative barrenness without batting an
eye, that he'd put up with Nollie's dreadful

housekeeping and cooking rather than hurt the old man who had looked after him since he was a boy.

She paused outside Billy's pen, fingering a few silky strands that had caught in a section of barbed wire. "What sort of man owns a ranch this size and lets an old goat like you decorate the entrance, Billy? When the wind's right, they can probably smell you all the way to the main house."

Wint greeted her with the news that she was dining out. "It's my poker night. Roane sets in on the game now 'n then, but this time he's a-givin' it up to look after you."

Exasperated, Cleo tossed her knapsack into the corner, jeopardizing the fragile pastels she used for color notes. "Wint, if you want me out of the way, all you had to do was tell me. I can take myself into Guymon for dinner and a movie. Roane doesn't have to baby-sit me."

"Too late now. He'll be a-pickin' you up in half an hour. Go gussy up and rake the straw out o' yer hair. You sure you been tumblin' around in them hills all by yourself?"

The old man leered, and Cleo made a rude remark about billy goats and dirty old men before stalking off to her eight-by-ten-foot bedroom. If the jars of pickled eggs, pigs' feet and red hot sausages Wint had lined up on the counter were anything to go by, she'd just as soon not hang around. Any card party that required a case of beer and that much indigestible food would be too wild for her taste.

By the time Roane drove up—the pickup truck had been supplanted by something dark and low and quietly elegant—Cleo had showered, shampooed the wild grass seed from her hair and dressed in her one remaining decent outfit, a cowl-necked dress of gray wool jersey that skimmed lightly down her body to swirl around her knees. She tossed a hand-loomed shawl across her shoulders and snatched up her purse.

In the cramped living room, her eyes met Roane's across the battered card table. "Now feed her up good, Roane," Wint ordered. "You know women—the skinnier they be, the meaner they be."

"I won't bring her back until I've sweetened her up for you, Wint," Roane agreed solemnly, and Cleo shook her head in exasperation at the pair of them. How far did a woman have to travel to get away from patronizing men? Still, if she had to choose between the sort she'd found out here in the panhandle and what she'd left behind, there was no contest.

"You're sure you wouldn't rather stay here and dine on Penrose Hots and beer?" Roane asked solicitously as he settled her in the leather-scented interior of his car. "The boys could always make room for another player."

"My stomach might take it, but I'm not sure my ears could. I've heard Wint when the cards were running against him."

He backed carefully away from the clutter of animal enclosures and turned toward the state road. "When did you hear that? There hasn't been a game since you've been here."

"The last time I was here, I saw Wint sneak out after Mama and Daddy were asleep, and I followed him. They played five-card draw in a barn, and I listened in and wished I'd brought a pencil and paper so I could write down all the new words and phrases I learned. I looked in the dictionary when I got home, but most of them weren't listed.''

Roane laughed, and the sound of it was oddly disturbing. "Colorful, huh?"

"In shades of blue." The radials sang quietly over the pavement, accompanied only by the syncopated rhythm of the tar patches. Cleo caught a tang of some elusive aftershave and breathed deeply to draw it into her lungs. There was something exhilarating about being there, in this place, with this man. *Careful, Cleo—this one doesn't even bother to pretend. You don't want to get caught in that particular trap again, do you?*

The long, low supper club on the outskirts of Guymon was dimly lit and surrounded by luxuriant shrubs that reached the heavily timbered eaves. A uniformed boy appeared to park the car, and Roane led Cleo inside, where they were met by a tuxedoed maître d'. From the note of surprised pleasure in the several greetings they received on their way to a secluded table, it was obvious that Roane was both a known and an unfamiliar figure.

"Sorry I didn't stop for introductions. If you'd like—"

"No, it's fine. There's no point in meeting people I'll never see again, is there?" Cleo glanced around her with interest. It was evidently either a private or a very exclusive club. It could almost have been back East except for the silver-tipped longhorn skull mounted over the bar.

Her eyes returned to Roane in time to catch a flicker of some indecipherable expression on his face; then he was distracted by the waiter. The business of ordering drinks dispensed with, Roane once more turned his attention to her.

"So tell me, how did you occupy yourself today? Feeding the livestock and washing a few more windows?"

Toying with the margarita the waiter had placed before her, Cleo laughed. "One window washing per trip is my limit. As for the chickens, I'm just trying to figure a way of using some of those iridescent tail feathers in my weaving."

Roane shook his head. "Wint doesn't weave too, does he? I can't figure out why a man would keep a penful of roosters. They don't lay, don't fight, aren't going to wind up on his table, and they're noisier than a flock of guinea hens."

"They're pets."

"Like old Billy?" Roane taunted, a gleam of amusement crinkling his eyes. He tossed back his drink and stood. "Dance with me. I didn't bring you all the way to Guymon tonight to talk about Wint's livestock."

Her mind formed a question that faltered on her lips. What *had* he brought her there for? He was under no obligation to entertain her. The previous night's dinner had satisfied the demands of hospitality.

She moved into his arms, and he held her easily, not attempting to tighten the embrace. The music was blatantly romantic, the plaintive country ballad counterpointed by a sophisticated piano, and it occurred to Cleo belatedly that she was skating on dangerously thin ice. At least half a dozen couples were dancing, but in the red-brown gloom of the discreetly lighted room, they might as well have been alone. Warmly cocooned in Roane's arms, she closed her eyes and moved to the music.

Roane turned deftly, pivoting her against his inner thigh, and she was unable to repress a small gasp. *It's only flesh, for God's sake, Cleo—just another body. We all have one, and Roane's is essentially no different from anyone else's.*

Without knowing quite how or when, Cleo found herself molded tightly to the resilient hardness of Roane's torso. Her forehead was tucked into the hollow of his neck, and her hand was folded intimately in his. The music flowed through her with syrupy slowness. It was unending. Time hung suspended in a three-foot square as they swayed imperceptibly together. She inhaled raggedly, breathing in the essence of tobacco, good woolens and clean, healthy maleness, with an elusive tang of some masculine fragrance that ought to be outlawed.

"The music's stopped," Roane rumbled softly in her ear, and she blinked her way back to earth.

His smile was gentle and knowing, and Cleo moved quickly away, thankful for the dim lights. Since when had she started behaving like an adolescent with her first crush? Given a basic knowledge of biology,

she should have known better than to get
herself into such tantalizing situations. In
fact, if she didn't take herself in hand, she
was apt to wind up as just another notch on
a cowboy's bedpost.

Cleo led the way back to their table, her
head high and her stride brisk. Roane held
her seat, smiled indulgently at her and allowed her to steer the conversation into impersonal channels. They spent a good deal of
time arguing over the menu before ordering. They discussed food in general, and
from there they went on to talk about the
problem Roane had at home.

"What about chili?" Cleo asked, nursing
her drink cautiously. "I thought that was a
staple out here."

"We reached an understanding about chili
just last month. Three times a week, not
three times a day. I ordered up meat, potatoes and an occasional vegetable, and you
saw the results. If I say anything, it's back to
chili again, and Nol's chili will blister paint."

"What about canned goods? Surely he
can open a can and heat it up." She toyed
with the foot of the cut-glass vase and tried

to ignore the fact that those lazy topaz eyes were moving over every visible inch of her.

"He'd be mortally insulted if I suggested he serve canned food."

The eyes were lingering on the area just above the table, and Cleo's hand fluttered to her breast, wondering if the slit below the modest cowl neck was gaping open. The touch of her own hand on her breast, even through the soft wool jersey, had a decided effect on her, and she welcomed the intrusion of the waiter with their salad course.

Over a delicately seasoned endive salad with the unexpected touch of grated raw peanuts, Cleo asked about the various grasses and roadside weeds. "The colors are incredible—your wheat, if that's what's sprouting just now in all those fields, is pretty, but the section over to the left of the driveway, just past that old windmill, is my favorite. I adore pink grass."

She adored pink tenderloin as well, she assured him when he inquired if the beef was too rare for her. Before she had polished off her substantial serving, she had learned more than she really cared to know about sand sage, little bluestem, greater bluestem, and

sand love grass. Over a Cointreau-laced tri-
fle, she heard about blue grama and buffalo
grass, and not until they were sipping their
coffee did she notice the gleam of laughter
lurking behind Roane's grave facade.

"I think that pretty well covers the local
grasses unless you're interested in Bermuda
or Saint Augustin. Now, you mentioned
some dried weeds—but maybe you'd like to
take a break before we get started on that
subject. It's pretty involved, especially if
you're interested in the various means of
propagation and eradication techniques
currently under st—"

"Forget I asked!" she pleaded laughingly. "I was just as fascinated by all the
mauves and pinky browns and those feathery gray things before I knew their given
names."

"You're sure, now? I'd hate like the devil
for you to get home and not be able to sleep
nights wondering which was lead plant and
which was saltbush." His fingers were caressing the rim of his saucer and then carefully following the projection of the spoon
handle, as if savoring each tiny irregularity
in the smooth roundness. Cleo's eyes clung

to the long, square-tipped finger, and she felt a delicious shudder pass through her.

"Hmmm?" She snapped out of her daze, aware that he was waiting for an answer to a question she hadn't heard.

"I said, would you care to dance again?"

Reluctantly, Cleo shook her head. Dancing under the influence of a few sips of margarita was bad enough; add two glasses of Cabernet Sauvignon, plus the Cointreau-laced dessert—plus a few other influences she'd rather not explore—and it was simply too risky. At least she knew her own limitations. "Let me just sit here and ruminate for now," she murmured. "Wake me up if I go to sleep."

Roane flashed her a quick grin. "Maybe now's the time to reintroduce the subject of our upcoming wedding."

Her eyelids flew open. "Our upcoming what?"

"If you'd like to make it a fancy society affair, I'll go along with you, but it seems a little wasteful to me. I figured we could drive into town one day next week and take care of the necessary legalities, and then, for a honeymoon, we might run over to Boise City. I could have you back home in time to cook lunch the next day, and then you and Nol can start divvying up your territory."

His expression was so absurdly guileless that she had to laugh. "It would serve you right if I took you up on it. Didn't anyone ever tell you it was dangerous to go around proposing marriage to strange ladies? Or have you always enjoyed sticking your head in lions' mouths?"

He shook his head dolefully. "What must I do to get you to take me seriously? Would you like to take a look at my bank statement? How about a reference from my doctor and three unsavory business acquaintances?"

"Sorry. I could never marry a man who didn't care for weeds in his pastures. Nothing personal—it's just that I prefer my dried arrangements to have a little more variety."

"Some women can't be satisfied. Give them alfalfa and they ask for pigweed." He sent her a woebegone look. "Then you're actually condemning me to a lifetime of caustic chili and watery soup?" He sighed wistfully. "Funny, you don't look heartless, but then I was always too naive to see the greed behind a pretty face. Just hopelessly, trusting, I guess.''

In a tone reeking with false sympathy, Cleo said, ''I'm terribly sorry. I've probably left an indelible bruise on your tender young heart, but in years to come, you'll forget me. As a matter of fact, I even thought about inviting a couple of my friends out as consolation. Reba's a whiz at managing—she'd straighten out your affairs in no time—and Debbie's cooking makes whimpering babes out of strong men.''

''You really think you can talk one of them into volunteering to marry a poor old bachelor who's halfway over the hill?'' He touched his jagged hairline with mock despair. ''Pretty soon I won't even have the options Wint has, but at least my teeth, such as they are, are all my own.''

Cleo pretended to consider. ''The only trouble is,'' she mused, ''they've both used up all their vacation time until after the first. Do you think your digestive system could survive another month of Nollie's boiled beef and paint thinner?''

Roane shook his head slowly. ''I seriously doubt it. I'm getting so I look forward to his coffee, and that's one of the first symptoms of terminal indigestion.'' One of his fingers absently touched the ring on her hand—an inexpensive dinner ring of silver and baroque gray pearl. As he stroked the contours, he said, ''Maybe we could find a way for you to help me out before you go, though—if you're willing to spare me a few minutes of your expert professional advice.''

He looked up at her with an earnestness that was almost convincing. The finger stopped playing with her ring, and his hand relaxed, accidentally covering her fingers where they lay on the heavy linen cloth. ''No—it's too much to ask. Forget I mentioned it. Forget me and my problems and go your carefree way.''

''Roane—'' Cleo shook her head half in exasperation. It was all just an elaborate joke...so why was she beginning to feel guilty? Resignedly, she asked, ''What did you have in mind? And don't give me any more of your sheepish looks, either. I'm serious. If there's something you think I can do, I'm willing—within reason. But if you want my help, you've got to stop joking around about marrying me. It was funny the first time, but if you must know, my sense of humor where men are concerned has long since worn thin.''

"If I said I was crushed, would you believe me? No? I thought not." His expressive mouth twisted in a grin, and he removed a flat silver case from his inner pocket. "I guess I'll just have to console myself with a good cigar."

By the time he had finished the ritual of unwrapping, stroking the sides, inhaling the pungent sweetness of the leaves and clipping the end, Cleo was fidgeting. In growing discomfort, she watched while he lighted it and allowed a curl of fragrant blue smoke to wind its way lazily up toward the ceiling duct.

He was doing it all deliberately; that much was obvious. The reason behind all this long, drawn-out ritual was less obvious. In fact, if she'd been pressed to come up with an answer, she'd have said he was stalling for time.

Which made no sense at all. Tightening up her usual husky Carolina drawl, she said, "Roane, if you don't mind, it's getting late, and we have quite a drive ahead of us."

Roane nodded to the waiter, and their cups were magically refilled. Cleo sighed impatiently. "Look, you might be immunized by Nollie's caffeine stew, but I didn't sleep all that well last night." She took a sip and scowled at him. Then, forcing her eyes to hold Roane's deceptively bland gaze, she said grimly, "I'm waiting." A joke could go only so far, and this one—if it *were* a joke— had gone far enough.

"It occurred to me that with your expertise, I might be able to cut the risk factor considerably when it comes to selecting a wife. You know, when a man reaches forty, his needs are pretty well cut and dried. With your help, I could interview several applicants, weed 'em out and come up with someone suitable—some levelheaded, capable woman who doesn't mind tackling a real challenge in exchange for bed and board."

Cleo stared at him in astonishment. He couldn't actually be serious, could he? Could any man possibly be that insufferably smug? She had a real weakness for deadpan humor, but she'd be the first to admit that it had its dangers, especially when dealing with a man she didn't really know.

"In that case, you can forget about my two friends," she murmured dryly. He might be a millionaire—he might even have graced a rodeo or two—but she wouldn't wish him on her worst enemy. He was either the quintessential male chauvinist, a cold-blooded opportunist or a fool. And whichever he was, the fact that he was so damned attractive only made him that much more dangerous.

"Fair enough," Roane replied blandly. "You provide the expert evaluation, and I'll provide the candidates. I think I can drum up one or two females who'd be willing to come out for Thanksgiving. Pete Myers, my ranch manager, can pick 'em up and fly 'em into Guymon, so at least the losers won't be out any pocket money."

"Hmmm. Which ones do you consider the losers and which the winner?"

"It occurs to me that I've just been slightly insulted."

"Oh, you noticed?" Cleo gave him a saccharine sweet smile. "How perceptive of you. Well, let me just say that any woman who chooses to sell herself short gets precisely what she deserves. And now, if you'll write up a list of specifications for the position, I'll look it over, and we can get started. I won't be here forever, you know," she added tartly.

"Hmmm—this is going to take some consideration." His fingers touched the hand she had jerked away moments earlier, and she snatched it away again.

Tilting her head, Cleo studied him skeptically. Was he pulling her leg, after all? A joke was a joke, but this was ridiculous! Maybe he and Wint, and even Nollie, had collaborated on an elaborate prank at her expense. But why? What was the point of it all? Surely he couldn't push it much further.

"If you're ready, I'd just as soon get out of here," he murmured.

She was more than ready. Too much wine, too much soft music and too much exposure to a man like Roane Gallagher could be hazardous to a girl's health. Once again, they ran the gauntlet of Roane's friends and acquaintances, and this time he paused to introduce her to half a dozen people.

"Hope you don't mind my not introducing you before," he said as they waited for the car to be brought around. The air was crisp and dry and comfortably chilly, and the rising moon edged a thin veil of clouds with iridescence. "Folks around here are the friendliest people you'll ever meet. If we'd stopped to speak on the way in, we'd have ended up pushing tables together and making a party of it, and that wasn't exactly what I had in mind for tonight."

Cleo deliberately refrained from asking the obvious question. She was no novice at steering clear of provocative subjects. She'd play along with him on this marriage-stakes charade up to a point, but if he thought he was going to involve her in anything more personal, then he was in for a rude awakening. "Thank you for the dinner. It was delicious."

"Don't mention it," Roane dismissed, casting her a look of cool amusement.

As the lights of town faded behind them, Roane asked her what she thought of no-man's-land, as the panhandle had once been called. Cleo stretched out her legs in comfort and leaned her head back as she began to relax again. Her guard had been raised and lowered so many times in the past few hours that she was exhausted. With increasing enthusiasm, she began to describe her reactions to dramatic contrasts to be found in the wide, wind-swept landscape.

"I love those sad old houses with their dilapidated windmills and the tumbleweed trapped against the foundations—and the old-style grain elevators that rise up like something from a John Steuart Curry painting. But there's also something so exciting about all the pumperjacks and drilling rigs and the shiny pipeline. Some of those irrigation rigs look like enormous mechanical praying mantises."

She found herself curled around on the seat, one foot tucked under her as she gestured eloquently with her hands. The wariness that had grown throughout the evening was forgotten, and that odd sense of rapport was back again.

"Lying out there on top of a hill, I can almost feel the thunder of buffalo hooves—do you know what I mean? Did you ever see that painting of the Indian listening to the telephone pole? I think it's called the talking wires, or something like that." Unconsciously, she allowed her gaze to dwell on the rugged profile that was silhouetted against the brilliant night sky. Had that long, slightly crooked nose, the high, sharp-edged cheekbones come from some far-distant American Indian ancestor? It could very well be, but she'd be willing to wager that the wicked sense of humor was pure Gallagher Irish.

Nodding, Roane said quietly, "I know the one you mean." He turned off the state highway onto a narrow county road, and it was some time before it occurred to Cleo to ask where they were going.

"Thought I'd show you something special. The poker game is probably just getting hot about now—we wouldn't want to break it up by showing up too soon. This way home takes us just a mile or so out of the way, and it's well worth seeing on a night like this."

Her imagination working feverishly, Cleo was quiet while he turned off on an unpaved road that climbed one of the low, dunelike hills. Just before they reached the top, he slowed and turned to her.

"Humor me. Close your eyes until I tell you to open them again, hmmm?"

"This is ridiculous! Oh ... all right." Just
as she was ready to dismiss the man as either
a joker or a narrow-minded reactionary, he
turned into a little boy with a gleeful secret.
Who—or what—*was* Roane Gallagher, anyway? She knew a moment's regret that she
wouldn't be around long enough to find out.

Four

"How are your shoes?" Roane asked as he opened the door and handed her out.

"Fine, thanks, and yours?" Cleo's eyes were still ostentatiously shut, and she shivered as the raw wind cut through the thin knit of her dress.

"Three straps and four-inch heels aren't exactly hiking boots." Before she realized what was happening, he had swept her up in his arms and was carrying her to the crest of the hill. Her eyes flew open as she protested.

"Ah-ah! Close your eyes," he warned. "You'll spoil my surprise."

"This is ridiculous." Unfortunately, what was meant to sound derisive came out sounding slightly breathless, and Cleo could have kicked herself for being so acutely aware of the arms that held her. The height of the hill was magnified a hundredfold by the addition of a pair of long, muscular legs, a narrow wedge of hips and a long, flaring torso. "Don't tell me this is the way Fay Wray got started," she grumbled.

He laughed, and the sound reverberated down her spinal column. With his arms tucked under her knees and around her back, she felt perfectly secure, but there were dangers, and then there were *dangers*. Roane's breath was a warm current of air on her cheek as he murmured, "King Kong never had it so good. Now close 'em, honey. We're almost there."

They began to move again, and for the first time, Cleo wondered what on earth he had to show her out here in the farthest corner of his enormous spread. "Now?" she asked as he came to a halt. She could feel the increased force of the wind as it swept up the hillside, carrying with it the subtle fragrance of the dried grasses.

Roane lowered her slowly to her feet, still holding her with one arm. He turned her so that she stood with her back against his sheltering body.

"Now."

She'd come to the conclusion that it would be a spectacular view of the moon, with perhaps a windmill silhouetted against it. Instead, she saw a series of small, irregular ovals reflecting the silvered sky upward from the dark, winding ravine.

"My favorite string of pearls," Roane said softly, his mouth only inches from her ear. "Your ring reminded me of it. Same shape, same color on a moonlit night like this."

"Roane, it's lovely! What are they? Where did they come from? I thought once you passed the Optima Lake region, this whole panhandle was high and dry."

"Not really. We're as drought prone as the rest of this part of the country, but then, sometimes it'll rain so long and hard that half of Cimmaron County winds up as Texas mud. That's when our playa lakes get filled up. The water can't soak in as fast as it comes down, so it gathers in low places and stays there until the water table gradually lowers enough to accommodate it.''

"You mean there are more of these things?''

"Hundreds of 'em.''

"They're beautiful. They really do look like a broken string of pearls. Thank you, Roane.'' She turned to smile up at him, and the ever-present wind blew her hair across his face.

Laughing, he brushed it from his eyes, but instead of releasing it, he held on, drawing her closer until his face was a dark blur silhouetted against the bright pewter sky.

With a dreamy sense of inevitability, Cleo surrendered herself to his kiss. It had to happen sooner or later, if only to defuse the tension that had been growing inside her.

His parted lips brushed over hers lightly. Once . . . twice. They settled with incredible gentleness, moving softly against her mouth until it opened. Even then he wasn't greedy. Nor was she. *Just one,* she promised herself—just this one kiss, and then I'll let him know I'm not interested.

While the chilly November winds pushed against them, he played with her, teased her, planted tiny kisses along the curve of her top lip and tugged gently at the bottom one until she could have screamed. Her fingers curled against his chest, and she forced herself to remain unresponsive.

What was he *doing?* Why was he taking all night about it? If he was going to kiss her at all, why didn't he do it properly instead of nibbling so cautiously around the edges? Stunned, she realized that what she was actually feeling was resentment—resentment that he was obviously not particularly interested in what she had to offer. And damn it, it wasn't as if he'd have another chance, either. Just one good, deep, soul-satisfying kiss and then she intended to keep out of his way for the duration of her visit.

And he wasn't even going to go for it! Trembling with the strength of her frustrated anger, Cleo jerked herself from his loose grasp and turned away, crossing her arms over her chest as the wind threatened to tear her shawl from her shoulders.

"Cleo—"

"I'm freezing! Let's go."

"Cleo, what's wrong?" His hand came down on her shoulder, and she ducked under his grip and stalked across the tufted hilltop to where the car was parked.

"Nothing's wrong. Why on earth should you think something was wrong?" Her voice was as brittle as an icicle. She let herself inside, huddling in the creamy leather bucket seat to wrestle her temper under control. How utterly disgusting to lose her cool over something like this. And she had. If there was one thing she prided herself on, it was self-honesty. Admit it—she was mad as hell because he hadn't been carried away by the touch of her lips. Her ego would much rather have had him panting and pleading instead of being so irritatingly calm and collected.

All right, so she was disappointed. Roane was an attractive man, and a woman couldn't help but respond. And damn it, *no* woman liked to discover that a man found her eminently resistible!

"Why do I get the feeling that I've offended you? Didn't you want to be kissed? Is that it?" He started the car and turned around on top of the hill, and Cleo caught a last glimpse of Roane's lakes.

Suddenly, it occurred to her how very childish she was being, and she relented. "Oh, Roane, I'm just being silly. I don't know what's the matter with me. Maybe I'm more tired than I thought. I'd been working flat out for weeks before I came out here, and the drive alone took three days of hard pushing. Maybe it's jet lag." She laughed ruefully. "Fifteen hundred miles at extremely low altitude."

Roane shot her a quick, searching look. He could have sworn she had wanted him to kiss her. After all, a man doesn't bring a woman miles out of the way on a night like this for the scenery alone. Maybe he should have pushed a little harder. Maybe she was interested in a quick affair to top off her ranch vacation. Dammit, if he'd taken it easy, it was only because she kept on sending out mixed signals. Either that or he'd lost what knack he'd had for reading a woman.

Gearing down for the steepest part of the grade, he glanced at her again. Good profile. Nice brow under that little bit of fringe, and the nose was everything a woman's nose should be. On another woman, that jaw might be considered too strong, but on Cleo it merely reflected a strength of character he'd sensed from the beginning.

It occurred to him with a feeling of pleasant surprise that he liked a forthright woman a damned sight better than the kind who was afraid to speak up for fear of offending him. He'd learned about the latter kind back at Stillwater twenty years before, when he'd made the mistake of moving out of the dorm and into a luxury apartment. He'd been a jackass, and he'd paid the price. Since then, he'd learned to downplay his assets, although it wasn't exactly easy to hide twenty-eight sections of prime land riddled with beef and assorted hardware.

Not that Cleo seemed all that impressed. Either that or she had got herself a pretty fine act. Pity she wasn't going to be around much longer, although he couldn't blame a woman for not wanting to hang around in that dump of Wint's. Maybe if he offered to put her up at the house...

As if what he had to offer was so much better, he acknowledged ruefully. It was ironic in a way. He'd grown up in that empty icebox on the hill with a couple of tough old men. One had taught him all he ever knew about caring, and the other had considered the road to hell paved with inner-spring mattresses and fancy plumbing. If there'd ever been a tender side to Dave's hard-bitten nature, he hadn't revealed it to his only son. Once on his own, Roane had overreacted and shot the works, from the Maserati to the penthouse apartment. By the time he was twenty, he was married to a gold-digging little hooker who liked her bread buttered on both sides, and by the time he was twenty-three, he was divorced, disenchanted and determined to make it on his own. That ambition, at least, had won the old man's approval.

Beside him, the woman stirred restlessly. He caught a whiff of her subtle, clean-smelling perfume. Cleo. Cleopatra? God, it probably was. Still, on her, it looked good. Maybe he shouldn't have kissed her. Be a damned shame to acquire a taste for something like that, only to have it snatched away. How much longer did she have? A week? Two weeks? Might be interesting to see what developed before she went back home.

Turning onto the state road again, Roane considered taking the long way around and stopping by the house for drinks. Ten to one the game would still be going on at Wint's, and she'd just feel uncomfortable having to climb all over Nol and Rado and Josie to get to her room.

"Would you like to stop by the house for a nightcap?"

Cleo glanced at him guardedly. He'd been silent ever since they left the hill, and she'd wondered uncomfortably if he were regretting taking her out. Most of the inexplicable anger had drained from her by now, leaving her feeling oddly tired. After all, she'd walked miles that day, at least half of it uphill. "I don't think so, thanks. Sorry if I've been acting like a spoiled brat, Roane. I really don't know what came over me." She could at least be as honest with him as she was with herself. She owed him that much.

"Don't mention it. Does that mean our engagement is back on?"

Laughing helplessly, she allowed her head to fall back on the headrest. "Roane, I'll probably regret it for the rest of my days, but no, I won't marry you—although it would

serve you right if I did. I'd heard you west-
erners did everything on the grand scale, and
if that's an example of your practical jokes,
I'd have to agree." At least his wacky sense
of humor had the effect of restoring her
equilibrium. "If I started batting my eyelashes and making noises like a bride, you'd
be scrambling around like mad trying to pull
in your horns."

Shifting down into second, Roane turned
in through the gates and then shifted back
into third with smooth efficiency. He allowed his hand to rest absently on the knob
while his high forehead gathered in a frown.

She was absolutely right—wasn't she?
God, he must have left his brains in his other
hat! Over the past fifteen years or so, he'd
avoided some of the cleverest man traps west
of the Mississippi, and some of them had
been baited with real gourmet fare. Now he
unaccountably found himself stringing along
with a loco old beekeeper, handing a woman
he'd known only a couple of days a gold-
plated invitation to take him for all he was
worth. She could skin him alive and throw
away the carcass and he'd have only himself
to thank.

That wily, scheming little runt had started it all, of course, with his outrageous plan to feather his own nest. Roane probably needed his head examined, but one look at the bait and he'd gone along with it. She'd been mad as hell, all red-faced, with her hair every whichaway. She'd jacked that damn-your-hide chin of hers up in the air and leveled him with a pair of the steadiest gray eyes he'd ever run across, and then she'd laughed. Something had happened to him then. He didn't know exactly what it was, but she was beginning to get under his skin.

Parking upwind of Billy's pen, he turned to her, leaning against his door. "But meanwhile, what am I going to do? Nollie's not about to step down as chief cook and bottle washer. Wint's right—my only chance to get some relief without mortally offending him is to bring home a wife. So if you're sure I can't tempt you, I guess I'll just have to take you up on your offer."

For a minute, Cleo was genuinely puzzled. Then, remembering their earlier bantering, she shook her head slowly. "You know what? You're nuts. Maybe if you were twenty instead of forty, I might believe you, but—"

"When I was twenty, I already had a wife," he said quietly, any trace of teasing gone from his deep voice. *Good God, why on earth did I tell her about that? I doubt if anyone around here ever knew about Chrissy. Dave damned sure never told a soul!*

Cleo twisted the ends of her shawl. Why that should come as any great surprise to her, she couldn't have said. After all, what did she know about the man? "I see the trucks are still here," she mumbled awkwardly. "I can slip in the back door—it leads directly to my room."

"We could go up to the house for a while," Roane offered diffidently. "I might try my hand at making hard-boiled coffee."

Her smile was pasted on. "Thanks, Roane, but I'd better turn in. I walked for miles today, all the way to the far side of the pasture where that huge cow with the sweet face lives. Right now, I'm beginning to discover muscles I didn't even know I had."

"That sweet-faced cow, as you call it, is a Simmental bull," he said dryly. "You either need glasses or a lesson in basic biology.

Maybe I'd better give you a guided tour tomorrow."

"Really, that's not necessary," she assured him hastily, gathering her purse and fumbling for the door latch. "I promise not to wave any red flags and to run from any cow that looks like a bull."

"You run and you're inviting pursuit. Just don't climb any fences or open any gates," Roane warned her. "Anyway, we'll need to get together so that we can work on the specifications." At her puzzled look, he elaborated. "For a wife." His artless expression was somehow not very convincing as he reminded her that she had offered to help him.

"Roane, this has gone far enough."

"You *did* offer, but if your promises don't mean anything..." He sounded so disappointed she was tempted to laugh.

The temptation faded. Peering at him skeptically, she wondered what had happened to all that mental affinity they had shared the night before. Had she only imagined it? Now she couldn't even scratch the surface of those honey-colored eyes. He *had* to be joking. Surely he couldn't be serious.

And damn it, why had he kissed her? Noblesse oblige? Had he thought she expected it of him? Just because a man buys a woman dinner and dances with her once, it doesn't automatically follow that he has to make a pass.

Oh, the devil with it! If he wanted to play games, then she'd go him one better. "You want my help in finding a woman to marry? You've got it. You provide the candidates, I'll set up the weeding-out procedure." Let him turn himself wrong side out trying to scramble out of that one. "But we'll have to work fast if we're going to get you squared away before I go back home. Make me a list of any personal likes and dislikes; give me an idea of what the job will entail and what the benefits are. Salary, of course—that's personal allowance as well as working capital— and what about paid vacations? Also, staff assistance—what type and how much can she expect? Is this a dead-end job? Is there an adequate retirement plan? What are the chances for advancement? Will any possible promotions be straight line or lateral? What are the hours, and are the specified duties subject to—"

"Whoa there, honey!" He laughed softly and covered the small fists that were, for some obscure reason, clenched in her lap. "I get the picture. Can we get together on it tomorrow night? I've got an appointment in Boise City in the afternoon, but I should be back in time for dinner. We can go over it then. In fact, you might enjoy going with me. If you can stand the excitement of so much high living, we'll make it another night on the town."

"Oh, I don't think so, Roane." Cleo kept her voice even. One part of her wanted to claw that self-satisfied grin right off his lean, weathered face, and the other part of her wanted to grab at his offer with both hands. What a maddening man! She schooled her voice to a casual coolness. "If you're determined to go on with this foolishness, drop by the trailer when you have a few minutes and we'll discuss the particulars."

He studied her silently for what seemed an ice age, and then he nodded slowly. "All right, Madam Personnel Director. Let's see just what sort of woman you think I need."

Against a background of raucous snorts, profane outbursts and rowdy laughter from the other end of the trailer, Cleo lay awake and compared Roane Gallagher to the man who had had such a powerful hand in shaping her life. The bitterness had long since worn off. She could think about Doug Parkins now without feeling a fierce compulsion to break something.

They were two different species—the rugged, hardworking rancher and the thin, clever New Englander she had lived with and supported for almost three years. She had met Doug in her sophomore year at the university. Trying for an art degree, she had been supplementing her small scholarship with work in the admissions office and waitressing at one of the town's better restaurants. Against great odds, she'd even managed to build up a modest savings account.

Doug had been a senior. She'd met him one morning in the office, and that very night he'd taken a date to the restaurant where she worked. The next day, he'd turned up in the office again, and from then on, he had waged a campaign she had found impossible to resist. In the first place, no one had ever sent her flowers before. When, on her twenty-first birthday, he had literally showered her with a cascade of dried, scented rose petals and then handed her twenty-one rosebuds—the deep red ones, with the longest stems—she'd laughed, then cried and then laughed again. He'd followed that up by taking her out to the restaurant where she worked and ordering the most expensive thing on the menu.

Within four months, he was sharing her two-room apartment. Within a year and a half, she was working full-time and attending one night class a semester, and her savings account was a distant memory. Doug was perpetually buried under law books, slogging away with grim determination. There had been no time for roses and nights out by then, and no money, either, but Doug had assured her that he'd make it up to her. She'd never have to work another day in her life once he got through law school. As soon as he passed the bar exam, or even before, if she preferred, they'd be married. Then it would be her turn to get her degree.

She'd believed him. He was so earnest, so clever, and surely no man had ever worked as hard as he had. When she'd quit school altogether and no longer been eligible for her part-time job in admissions, she'd landed the job in the personnel office at Rand's. It had meant getting up before daylight and commuting to Burlington, because moving had been out of the question for Doug, and leaving him was just as impossible. Who'd be there to see that he ate decent meals? That he had a clean shirt to wear to class? That he managed to get at least four hours sleep a night?

His parents had come down for graduation. Douglas, Senior, was thin and clever, too, and his wife was an expensively dressed woman with incredibly sad eyes. The girl with them was named Hannah. She was literally the girl next door, and her father was senior partner of a small, prestigious law firm back in New London. She wasn't pretty, but she obviously idolized Doug, who ignored her for the most part. All of which made it all the more stunning when two days after graduation, Cleo came back to the apartment to find all Doug's things missing. She almost missed the note, which stated simply that he and Hannah were being married that afternoon and going back to Connecticut with his parents.

The numbness of shock had worn off all too soon, leaving her heartbroken, furious, vengeful and insecure, in that order. She'd stuck with her job in spite of having told everyone that she'd be leaving soon to be married. With car payments to make and no savings left, she'd had little choice. She'd had to buy the secondhand car to commute to her job. Doug had gone with her to pick it out, and it was only a fluke that it had been in her name—he'd been in class when she'd signed the bill of sale. Aside from remarking a few times that women were invariably taken advantage of by mechanics, he'd let it ride.

Taken advantage of! And to think that at the time she'd appreciated his concern. He was lucky she hadn't hired a bounty hunter to track him down for her. After three years and all those meals she had cooked. After all the washing and ironing she had done, the darning, the buttons sewn on, and even, heaven help her, the shoes she had polished when he'd stayed up studying all night and had time only to shower and grab a cup of coffee before dashing off to class. And what had she had to show for all her sheep-brained self-sacrifice? A rusty sedan that needed a ring job, a pair of worn-out track shoes—men's size ten—and a subscription to Forbes that had two months to run.

Plus an iron-bound determination never to allow herself to be used again, she added grimly. She had dug in her heels and set her sights on Rand Smith's chair. She was good at her job, and she wasn't afraid of work. The next few years had held no room for self-pity. She'd transferred to a small college and changed her major to business, and she'd gotten her degree the hard way, by going to class every night and getting up at five to study.

By the time she'd received two promotions, she had gotten over the feeling of inadequacy that had followed the hurt and the anger. She knew damned well she was attractive, and what's more, she was smart. And anyway, she'd have been miserable married to Doug. Recently, she'd heard that he had divorced Hannah and was with a larger firm, living in New York and edging his way cleverly into politics. She'd been merely a rung on his ladder—one of the lower rungs, at that.

Well, dammit, she'd long since dusted his footprints off her back, and she wasn't going to lean over for any man again. If Roane wanted to play, then she'd go along with him—up to a point. At least they both knew the rules of the game. Then she'd take her marbles and go home, and on the off chance that he was actually serious, he could settle down with whichever poor fool was willing to marry a man under such cold-blooded circumstances.

By the time Cleo had cleared away the ruins of the previous night's poker game, the wind had dropped, and the sun had warmed up the day to a respectable sixty-four degrees Fahrenheit, with an even higher temperature expected before the unseasonable heat wave ended. Wint was nursing a sour stomach and a more sour disposition, and after doing all she could for him, she deemed it best to clear out until he recovered from too much beer and indigestible food and too many losing hands.

Tucking a grapefruit into her knapsack along with her drawing material, she headed for her favorite place on the ranch, a deep, winding ravine surrounded by fallow fields where dozens of varieties of grasses and weeds grew. On such a day, with plenty of sun and, for once, no wind, it should be almost balmy.

By the time she gauged it to be midafternoon, Cleo had designed a potentially stunning wall hanging. Now all she needed was a larger loom and space to set it up. She'd collected a sackful of dried weeds and grasses that she planned to incorporate in her weaving. Any left over would go in the lumpy weed pot she had made during her one foray into ceramics.

Rolling up her sleeves, she unbuttoned the top three buttons on her blue chambray shirt and lay back on the ground. Then she sat up and removed her shoes and socks and rolled up the legs of her jeans. It was four days before Thanksgiving, and the weather was practically tropical; she was determined to enjoy it while it lasted. Who knows, maybe she'd take home a nice suntan as a souvenir of her midwinter vacation.

She dozed until hunger roused her, and then she dug the grapefruit out of her bag and jammed her thumbnail into the stem end. She'd almost finished peeling it by the time Roane appeared over the rim of hills.

The horse he was riding was a big, ugly bay, with nothing to recommend him to Cleo's inexpert eyes except his size. Swinging out of the saddle, Roane looped the reins over a cottonwood branch and sauntered across to where Cleo sat cross-legged on the ground.

"Lunch?" He nodded to the partially peeled grapefruit in her hand.

"Unless you have something better to offer. I fell asleep and woke up starving."

He dropped down beside her to lift one of her hands for a closer examination. "You didn't wash your hands first."

"It's organic and biodegradable—it won't hurt you." She twisted off several segments and handed them over. "The vitamin C will take care of any germs."

He grinned and nipped the membrane with his teeth, and she wondered how she could have considered that one chipped tooth a weakness. The man had no weaknesses. He was invulnerable. And as if that weren't enough, there was the way he moved, the way he looked at her as if he owned the whole blooming restaurant and she were the special of the day. "I've never eaten grapefruit this way before," he murmured, tugging off half a segment with his teeth and chewing reflectively. He ducked his head, and his tongue caught at the juice that ran down his hand.

"It's sweeter like this," she confided.

He allowed his lazy glance to play over her, from her bare feet to her sticky hands to her sun-flushed face. "I think you're right."

Neither of them spoke until all the grapefruit was consumed, and then they both lay back on the warm earth. Overhead, a hawk caught an updraft and soared lazily. Cleo tuned out all thoughts of its real mission, preferring to concentrate on the beauty of its flight.

"Have you given any more thought to what we discussed last night?" Roane asked after several minutes had passed in comfortable silence.

Cleo had been making a real effort to direct her mind away from anything connected with Roane Gallagher. Unfortunately, she had about as much chance as the poor little field mouse that was going to wind up as a hawk's dinner any minute now.

Five

"If you mean about finding you a presentable female with a strong back and a weak mind, no, I haven't."

Roane rolled over on his side to study her, and with the sun blinding her, Cleo couldn't be sure of his expression. She couldn't even be sure she *wanted* to be sure. He said, "Why do I get the idea that you're not particularly enthusiastic about this enterprise?"

"Probably because I'm not," she retorted flatly. Something was digging into her back, and she shifted sideways and squirmed for a more comfortable position. Roane's shadowed eyes followed the small movement with interest, and she quickly subsided, the small discomfort forgotten.

"Are you against marriage in general or just mine in particular?"

"I'm not against marriage." She shrugged, crossing her arms over her chest.

"Then why all the sanctimonious disapproval?"

Rolling onto her side to face him across a distance of some few feet, her determination to remain coolly uninvolved began to crumble. She struggled valiantly to keep a stern expression on her face, but it was no good. Sanctimonious? *Her?* Her lips trembled, and when she caught his eye, she was lost. Laughing helplessly, she sat up and scratched the place on her back where the stalk of dried grass had made its mark. She surveyed herself derisively. Her hands were sticky with fruit juice and decidedly grubby from her morning of foraging. Her shirt tail was half in and half out of her ancient jeans, and her arms bore the imprint of the rough pasture as well as the marks of a briar or two. A varied collection of seeds was embedded in her damp, sun-flushed skin, and what wasn't represented there was no doubt caught in her tangled hair.

"Somehow I'd never considered myself sanctimonious," she confessed modestly. "Fastidious, certainly, but not—ouch!" She broke off when he caught at her arm and tugged her down on top of him. Before she could roll away, his arms closed over her, and he began to squeeze.

"Make fun of me, will you?" he growled. "How dare you laugh at my simple, homespun observations?"

His chin was digging into the top of her head, and her face was buried in his throat. The mingled scent of horse, dried grass and clean, healthy sweat that clung to him was impossibly intoxicating. "You're about as simple and homespun as I am sanctimonious," she gurgled. One of his hands had moved to her side to hold her still, and his fingers pressed into her ribs with catastrophic results.

"Roane, don't! Please—I can't stand it," she groaned, squirming under the solid weight of his body as he rolled over on top of her.

"What can't you stand?" he demanded, trapping her legs with his own when she tried to scramble out from under him.

"Tickling!" She had already moved his hand, and he didn't attempt to replace it, but the mere thought of his fingers at her ribs made her fall apart. "I'm horribly, terribly ticklish!" she panted.

Growing suddenly still, he considered her with a lazy, narrowing glint. "That's like handing a man a loaded gun," he suggested softly.

"But if a man's a gentleman, he won't use it," she pleaded.

His face went out of focus as his head began to lower. "Who said anything about being a gentleman?" he murmured just before his lips came down on hers.

Even if her nerves hadn't been trembling on the brink of chaos from the mere threat of being tickled, it would have been the same. The touch of his callused hands, the feel of his rock-hard weight pressing down on her and the masculine scent of his body combined to send her reeling off into space.

Add to that the coercive spell of his mouth, and she didn't stand a chance.

There was no nibbling around the edges this time. This time, he twisted his mouth with practiced ease to part her lips and then began to work his potent magic. Alternately advancing and retreating, demanding and seducing, he used tongue, teeth and lips to beguile her to the point where she was a helpless bundle of naked, aching need.

Reason was impossible. Panic erupted for one fleeting instant before that, too, went down under the spell of what was happening to her. Oh, God, it had never been like this before! She had been almost completely uninitiated before Doug, and after a while, when they had reached the point where sex was hurried and infrequent and seldom very satisfying for her, she had rationalized it easily. They were both always tired, always rushed. She had told herself that that was all that prevented her from responding to him the way she had those first few months together.

But even then, it hadn't been like this, she admitted shakenly.

"Undress me," Roane grated, lifting his body to enable her to reach the buttons on his shirt. He had already divested her of hers, and the top button of her jeans was lying somewhere in the bed of grass beneath them.

"Roane, this isn't very smart," Cleo protested weakly. Her fingers were feverishly attacking his buttons, but she found it almost impossible to concentrate when his teeth were raking slowly back and forth over the dusky rose nipple showing through the lace bra that covered it. The sensation that shot through her body to gather in the pit of her loins couldn't have been more acute if he'd been touching her bare skin.

His shirt unbuttoned, he was forced to sit up so that she could pull it down over his arms, but instead of lying back down with her again, he continued to sit beside where she lay sprawled on the sun-warmed bed of grass. His eyes ranged over her, lingering on the delicate hollows of her collarbone, ranging lower to move palpably over her small, full breasts. With a single finger, he traced the line of her low-cut bra over the hills and valleys, and she struggled to resist the urge to pull him down on top of her.

He was magnificent! His muscular arms and shoulders swelled smoothly under a covering of glistening bronze skin, and the pattern of dark hair that swirled across his chest before arrowing downward made her fingers curl convulsively. His narrow waist was taut and lean, and his compact hips were no wider. It was all she could do to keep her hands off him, but she was determined not to take the initiative.

How absurd, she heard a derisive voice—hers?—exclaim. As if it made any difference in the long run who took the lead in something as inevitable as this. There was no future in any sort of a relationship between her and Roane. Their goals were totally at odds. Knowing as much, she could no more prevent herself from responding to him physically than the sun could help rising in the east.

With infinite slowness, he undid the remaining buttons on her jeans. The touch of his knuckles on the flesh of her belly was enough to send her up in smoke, but she forced herself to remain quiescent. When the last one was unfastened, he slipped a hand beneath her hips to lift her free of the soft denim.

Wordlessly, she clung to his eyes. Throughout the whole slow, dreamlike procedure, they had been darkening, until now they were hard nuggets of obsidian rimmed by molten gold.

He removed her bra then, and last of all, her briefs, and she lay there under the haze of a late-afternoon sky, savoring the heat of the wild, sun-warmed grasses and the contrasting coolness of the November air. The world outside this small, hidden ravine had long since ceased to exist; the physical world had narrowed down to consist of two people—a man and a woman.

When Roane reached out to grasp a handful of grass, she followed the movement with a dreamlike interest, as if she were a part of the very earth that cradled her deliquescent bones. Skimming off the dried seed heads, he held her eye as, slowly and deliberately, he sprinkled them over her body, taking great care in their placement. It was only when he broke off another feathery stalk and began methodically to brush

them away again, that she uttered a sound.
The tickling touch of the dried grass against
the skin of her abdomen made her breath
catch in her throat, and the feel of his eyes
on her body as they deliberately followed the
movement of the miniature broom was even
more devastating.

With infinite care, he brushed the tips of
her breasts, neglecting no part of the small
baroque crowns. Then he began to trace the
subtle midline downward to her navel. Exploring the tiny depression as if it were ex-
traordinarily fascinating, he began the
inexorable downward sweep again, until the
grass stem would go no farther. When it bent
under the challenge of the rougher terrain,
he tossed it aside, and then he gently lowered his lips.

The burning moisture of his kiss on her
body sent wave after wave of stunning sensation coursing through her and left her
shuddering weakly. Her fingertips bit into
the hard flesh of his shoulders as wordlessly
she urged him to end the sweet torture. It
was all wrong, here under the brazen sky,
with the wind blowing chaff across them and
the hawk soaring relentlessly overhead. It

was all wrong, and yet it was all so wonderfully right!

When she could take no more, she touched his head, and with the same swift sentience she had come to expect from him, he moved to gather her in his arms. Touching her lips with a restraint that trembled in every hard muscle in his body, he whispered her name over and over.

"Cleo, Cleo, Cleo." The words feathered against the corner of her mouth, and she parted her lips on a soft moan of pleasure. "You have no idea how very beautiful you are to me right now."

She tasted his words, savoring them as her hands moved over his back to the narrow hardness of his buttocks. When she encountered his belt and the smooth softness of his worn whipcords, she looked up in time to catch his provocative grin.

"I've seldom been accused of being overdressed for the occasion, but this is one time when I plead guilty. If you'll excuse me a minute, I'll rectify the situation."

Her hands trailed from his as he stood up. Then, with her arms crossed above her head, she realized that she was being excited almost unendurably by the mere touch of the air currents on her body. He had sensitized her beyond belief! She watched him openly as he tugged off his boots and then stepped out of his clothes in one efficient movement. There was nothing at all self-conscious in her admiring look as he stood over her. It was a part of the overall rightness of the moment. His face and shoulders silhouetted by the golden haze that covered the sun, he towered over her until she held up her arms to him.

Responding to her impatience, he lowered himself beside her and began to kiss her with slow deliberation. It took only the tentative touch of her exploring hands on his body to dispel his control, however, and replace it with a fierce and hungry aggressiveness. His breath grew increasingly ragged, and when she touched a certain place at the base of his spine, a raw gasp escaped him, and he clutched her convulsively.

"Oh, God, honey, take it easy—it's been a while—"

It had been more than a while for Cleo. It had been forever. Nothing in her initiation of all those years before had prepared her for this heedless, compulsive need. She wanted to prolong the exquisite tension forever, and at the same time, she was driven to race headlong to the point of no return. Her hands sought him, and her thighs cradled him, and then there was no turning back.

"Cleo, honey—" he rasped, but she shook her head.

"No, don't talk," she ordered hoarsely. Her mind had long since shut down. All she knew now—all she *wanted* to know—was what was happening to her. There were no words. There was only this....

The words came later, after Icarus had reached the sun and burst into flames. After he had fallen to the earth again. It was the earth beneath her that prompted Cleo's first conscious thought and her subsequent words.

"There's a stick gouging my shoulder blade. If it goes on through, and you feel it scratching your chest, you might want to do something about it... Just a suggestion," she murmured. "I thought I'd mention it with my last breath of air."

Smiling drowsily, Roane eased himself off to one side, allowing her to draw the deep breath she'd been deprived of. "Sorry," he rumbled. "I told you—it's been a while. I forgot my manners."

As her thought processes slowly began to creak into action once more, it occurred to Cleo that that wasn't all he had forgotten— nor could she claim to have done any better. Swift mental calculations reassured her on one point, but she was aghast at her own ir- responsibility. Turning onto her side with her back toward him, she drew her knees up and stared out across the ravine. The red banks were alight with color from the setting sun, but she hardly noticed.

How on earth could she justify such a lapse? She had never gone in for casual sex. Until Doug, there had been no one. After Doug, there had been no one. There were too many dangers, both physical and emo- tional, and she had never found a man she considered worth the risk.

Until now. Until Roane Gallagher. "Oh, damn and blast," she whispered hopelessly. Of all the men she could have picked to be attracted to, why did it have to be one like him? It was a dead end. If she had a grain of sense, she'd get in her car the next morning, make a sharp right turn and go back to North Carolina. Unfortunately, she'd just proved conclusively that she didn't have a grain of sense.

"Cleo?" She knew from the direction of his voice that he was standing behind her.

"I don't want to discuss it," she said bluntly.

His short bark of laughter expressed disbelief. "I don't think you have a hell of a lot of choice, do you?"

At that, she rolled over and sat up, her knees still doubled up before her. Her shirt was within reach, and she snatched it up, and rammed her fists into the sleeves. The bra could wait. "If I don't want to discuss something, then I don't discuss it. It's that simple," she told him flatly. She wasn't exactly angry, and there was no point in pretending to be. Anyway, she was too straightforward to pretend convincingly. That, she realized sinkingly, could present a problem.

Squatting beside her, Roane reached for his boots. "Well, you can damn well listen to me discuss it, then."

She jumped up and stalked around, collecting her clothing. It took several minutes to find her left shoe, and by that time, Roane had put on both his boots and was on his feet. She studiously avoided looking at him, but there was no way she could ignore him. He was too large to ignore—too large and too threatening.

"Cleo, if you don't—"

"That does it!" Inside her jeans again, she felt more sure of herself. With one shoe on her foot and the other clutched in her hand, she jammed her fists on her hips and glared at him. "Roane, if you say one single word to me about this, I'm going home."

"I should hope so," he observed mildly. "Once that sun goes down, it gets cold as the devil out here."

"I don't mean Wint's trailer—I mean *home* home!"

"On the range?"

He ducked as she threw the shoe, and by the time he had retrieved it from the bottom of the ravine, she was giggling helplessly. She sobered when he knelt before her and took her foot in his hand.

"Roane, I meant it. What's done is done, and I won't pretend it wasn't as much my fault as yours, but it won't happen again. I may not be remarkably bright, but at least I learn from my mistakes."

He returned her level look, but as his head was against the fading light, she hadn't a hope of reading his expression. "And you consider what we just shared a mistake?"

She nodded. "For me, it was. For you—" She shrugged. "I doubt that it mattered one way or the other."

He started to speak and then seemed to think better of it. Tying her shoe, he stood and reached for her hand, and she allowed him to pull her up. "Come on. I'll give you a lift."

"I can walk." She shook off his hand as soon as she was on her feet.

Impatiently, he said, "I know you can walk, dammit. So can I if I have to, but you're a long way from home, and it'll be dark in a few minutes. I don't intend to spend the night wondering if you're still stumbling around out here in your shirt-sleeves!"

Unlooping the reins, he walked the ugly stallion over beside her, and she allowed herself to be boosted up. He handed her her knapsack, and then he swung up into the saddle. She had no choice but to hang onto him. Closing her eyes as she absorbed the warmth of his big body, she wondered if she was going to have the courage to get out of there before it was too late.

Wint had driven his battered pickup to Texhoma when she got up the following morning. He'd rapped on her door and asked if she wanted to go, but she'd begged off. She'd awakened on the same endless treadmill that had put her to sleep the night before, and like a tattered merry-go-round, it started up again as soon as she heard the truck drive off.

How had he found her? Why hadn't he gone to Boise City? Had he actually been looking for her, or was he just out riding fence?

Was she in love with him? She couldn't be. It was too soon.

On the other hand, she had never reacted to any man the way she had to Roane. Was she *potentially* in love with him? Putting it that way, she had to answer in the affirmative. If liking a man, respecting him and being enormously attracted to him physically held the potential for loving, then she couldn't deny it. And there was that strange, intimate way they had of picking up on each other's thoughts. She had an idea that if they both let down the barriers, it would develop even further.

The barriers would stay up. What had happened the previous day had simply happened. Given the circumstances, maybe it had been inevitable, but that didn't mean she was going to repeat it.

She'd cut her vacation short. Thanksgiving was coming up, and Wint had wistfully mentioned turkey and corn-bread stuffing several times. She couldn't let him down, but as soon as that was over, she was getting out of there. Every mile she put between herself and Roane Gallagher meant that much more of a safety factor. By the time she got as far as Tennessee, she'd have forgotten him. At least she'd have forgotten his magnetic appeal for her. Or at least she'd be far enough away so that she couldn't make a fool of herself for the second time in her life.

* * *

In the cold, cluttered office, Roane tilted his chair back precariously and idly tapped a pencil against his teeth. He'd called Shoemaker first thing to explain about missing that appointment the previous day. After that, he hadn't accomplished a damned thing. Every time he came to his office, there was another stack of paper work to wade through. At this rate, he'd drown in the damned stuff before help arrived. He'd hired a bookkeeper the month before, but he'd had to wait for the fellow to work out his notice. Meanwhile, he'd tried to keep abreast of the most pressing things, but it was uphill work. Especially when the government sent out a ream of paper on every subject faintly pertaining to agriculture or oil production.

Especially, he added with an exasperated sigh, when his mind kept going back to the day before.

Wint's truck rattled past, and he stared after it absently. The boys were working on the tub grinder out beside the machine shop. Crippled hands or not, Wint still knew more about the older equipment than most of the younger men. He generally stopped by after making the rounds of his bees, hoping to trade a shot of advice for a little gossip.

That meant she'd probably be alone. With the clouds piling up, she wouldn't be out hiking that day. He could go over there . . . On the other hand, she'd threatened to leave if he brought up what had happened between them, and she'd be just pigheaded enough to stick to her word.

And dammit, he didn't want to scare her off now. Maybe he could pretend he thought Wint was there and stop by to see him.

No, that was out. One look in those steady gray eyes and he'd probably turn beet red and blab out the truth. The woman could read him too well. They'd both be thinking about the same thing, and the whole damned ball game would be over before he could pull his foot out of his mouth. How the hell did you handle a woman like that? He'd never run across the problem before.

A cackle of laughter carried from the back of the house. Nollie's. Evidently, Wint had opted for the warmth of the kitchen instead of the increasingly raw wind out back. It was the only room in the place that *was* warm, and that was only because Nol wouldn't give up that cast-iron relic he cooked on. All the oil and gas in the country and he had to use wood!

Roane raked a hand through his dark, untidy forelock. One of these days he was going to have to do something about the drafty old barn. Even with most of his working capital either tied up in Gal-Way or earmarked for new equipment, he could well afford to level the place and start over.

No! Hell, he didn't want to do that. As miserable and cheerless as it was, it was still home. With an impatient gesture, he shoved back his chair and moved across to the window. He didn't know what he wanted. For the first time since he could remember, he didn't know what the devil he wanted! At first the challenge of going in with Hal Wayland to get Gal-Way Equipment off the ground had been enough. That done, he'd been considering the tax impact of selling controlling interest back to Hal when Dave had had his attack. Since then, the matter had been shelved.

Now, all of a sudden, he found himself with time to stop and deliberate, and all he could think about was a stubborn female with an irreverent sense of humor and a body that set him on fire. Dammit, he was old enough to know better! How did he get himself into such a fix? The trick now was to get himself out of it.

A hard gust of wind rattled the wavy glass panes in their frames, and he turned away impatiently. The real trick was to keep her there without spooking her until he had time to figure just what the hell was going on in his mind. Crossing to the phone, he dialed briskly. The phone rang four times. He was on the point of slamming it down—it had been a stupid idea, anyhow— when someone answered.

"Hello, Marsha? Roane Gallagher." He listened to a spate of reproaches and recriminations without bothering to offer any excuses. When it was over, he said, "Listen, honey. I've invited a few people out for Thanksgiving. If you've recovered from your last visit—No, I haven't had time to worry about it—Well, yes, but—"

A large booted foot thumped impatiently against the desk leg. "It's up to you, honey. Take it or leave it. If you want to come, I'll have my plane at the airport at four on Wednesday.''

He hung up and dialed again. By the time he had made the last call, he felt considerably more relaxed. Stupid or not, he had committed himself. Now all he had to do was to ride it out and see what developed.

Correction. Now all he had to do was to see that Cleo didn't back off and leave him stuck in the middle of a mess.

Leaning back in the swivel chair Dave had worn the finish off years ago, he took a cheroot from a box on the cluttered desk and allowed a slow, speculative grin to spread across his face.

Six

"Don't be absurd! I haven't the slightest intention of doing anything of the kind. Why should I?" Cleo looked up from the small hand loom she was working on to frown at the man lounging in the doorway. "Either come in or get out. You're letting in a draft."

Roane eased himself inside and closed the door behind him. He glanced around the crowded room diffidently until, with an impatient oath, Cleo uncurled her long legs and got to her feet, laying the loom on the heap of yarn that spilled all over the coffee table.

"You may as well sit down," she invited grudgingly, gathering up the rest of the yarn she had unpacked earlier. With the weather closing in, she couldn't get out and walk off her restless energy, and she'd been forced to seek other outlets.

"Look, Roane, if you've landed yourself with a bunch of house guests, that's your problem. Me—I've already made my plans. I'm going to be baking turkey and corn-bread stuffing and sweet potatoes and all the things Wint likes best. I've got pies in the oven right now, and I'm not about to walk out and let them burn." She stuffed the col-orful yarn back into the hatbox she used as a carrier and tried to ignore the look on his face. She owed him nothing.

"I don't blame you for not wanting to bother with me and my problems, Cleo. I guess I just didn't know where else to turn. It occurred to me that since you were partly responsible for my predicament, you might feel obligated to—"

"I'm *what?*" His look of harried inno-cence was too much for her. "Roane, you're the most incredible man I've ever met," she declared, torn between exasperation and amusement.

"Look, I know we were only kidding around—I mean about running a few heifers through the squeeze and checking them out. The trouble is, I'd already invited my business partner out from Tulsa, and it occurred to me that the girls might sort of round out the party, and I just sort of got carried away. Before I stopped to think it through, I'd called and invited a couple of lady friends out here for Thanksgiving."

"Oh, you poor, mad, impetuous fool," she jeered pityingly. His attempt at self-effacement wasn't wholly successful, but Cleo gave him credit for trying.

"Yeah, I guess I went a little overboard, but to tell the truth, I'm kind of rusty when it comes to socializing," he admitted wistfully. "It's been so long since I've had time to think about anything except work."

"Bring on the violins. Roane, in just the few days I've known you, you've entertained me in your home, you've taken me out to dine," Cleo stated, counting off the two events on her fingers. She stopped abruptly, but it was too late. The words that hovered in the air between them were as plain as a glowing neon sign, and it was perfectly obvious that Roane was as conscious as she was of what had come next.

The door burst open, letting in a gust of rain and cold air, and Wint stood on the doormat, looking from Cleo's stricken face to Roane's unnaturally red one. "You come to steal my cook away from me, boy? Take her and you'll have to take us both. Smell them pies a-bakin'? I told you that gal could cook!"

Diving headlong into the reprieve, Cleo glared derisively at her great-uncle. "And how would you know?" she snapped. "You'd never tasted any of my cooking before last week."

"Carolina gals is brought up right," the old man announced smugly.

"Well, Roane's invited himself a couple of Oklahoma gals for Thanksgiving. I assume they're equally well brought up, so that lets me off the hook." Flinging a triumphant look at both men, she stepped over Roane's muddy boots to get to the oven. A rush of warm fragrance filled the room as she cracked the door to check on the progress of her two pies, and she snatched the hot pad and eased them out onto the improvised cooling racks.

"Oh, my, don't that fair make your mouth water?" Wint groaned. He shucked off his yellow slicker and tossed it into a corner. "With a little bit of coffee to wash it down, Roane and me just might be able to force down a slab o' that mincemeat." He turned to the younger man. "She put coconut and brandy in it," he confided.

Cleo shook her head in resignation as she moved efficiently around the cramped kitchenette. Putting the kettle on to boil, she cut into one of the hot spicy pies and then reached into the refrigerator for the cream she had whipped earlier. A few minutes later, she turned and presented each of the men with a king-size serving of mincemeat pie. "You'll get your coffee when it's ready," she announced flatly.

Outside, the wind-driven rain beat against the metal sides of the trailer. The windows were steamed up, and the cluttered interior was warm and cozy and inviting. The untidy evidence of her weaving vied for space

with a half-finished game of checkers and
the racks Wint was repairing for the supers
on his bee boxes. Cleo thought of the gaunt,
empty old house on the hill, and in spite of
herself, she felt her resolutions begin to
crumble.

"What kind is the other one?" Roane
asked hopefully, scraping the florid design
on the bottom of his plate.

Cleo's flinty gray eyes slid away from the
wistful look on his rugged face. They
touched on a small tear at the corner of his
pocket, and she tried to ignore the stunning
masculine impact of the man. Dammit,
Roane Gallagher could buy a dozen baker-
ies and a whole shirt factory and never feel
it. She didn't have to feel so sorry for him.

Plunging her hands into dishwater, she
allowed Wint to answer for her. "It's
pun'kin. An' be danged if she didn't cook
the seeds and salt 'em down, too, and you
know what? They ain't half bad! I wuz goin'
to feed 'em to my chickens."

Shaking her head ruefully, Cleo admitted
defeat. They had ganged up on her—two
little boys, one seventy-five years old and the
other one forty. How could they do this to

her? Here she had prided herself on being so levelheaded and pragmatic, and all of a sudden she was being blatantly manipulated by a pair of hungry-eyed con artists.

"All right, enough of your nose-to-the-windowpane pathos," she growled. "You win! What do you want? A pie? Two pies? A turkey? You want me to sweet talk Nollie into letting me cook the whole blasted Thanksgiving dinner for you?" She planted her fists on her hips and faced the two men. At least they had the grace to look guilty—as well they should!—shoveling in the last of her mincemeat pie while they cheerfully blackmailed her into spending her holiday vacation in that great ark of a kitchen.

"Now, Cleo, you know we—" Wint began, but Roane interrupted him. The quick glance that passed between the two of them wasn't lost on her, but she didn't even try to interpret it. Whatever they'd cooked up between them, it wasn't going to work. She'd do exactly what she wanted to do—no more, no less.

"Well, you see, honey," Roane began diffidently, and she cut him off.

"Skip the sweet talk. Just spit it out. Tell me what you want from me and I'll give you my terms." Ha! Just as she expected, that brought them up short. "Oh, were you expecting me to donate my services?" she inquired sweetly. "I'm sorry—I just assumed it would be a business arrangement." She made an abortive attempt at fluttering her eyelashes and gave it up. One of these days, she'd get it down pat.

"Naturally, I don't expect to impose on your kindness," Roane informed her gravely. "If you'll just come up to the house and see to getting things ready—work something out with Nol so that we don't actually starve to death and do what you can to get three bedrooms looking halfway presentable—then you can name your price."

Turning away, Cleo hid her grin as she wrapped foil and then a towel around the uncut pumpkin pie. She slipped the bulky bundle into a paper bag and presented it to Roane. "Here, give this to Nollie with my compliments. Tell him there's more where this came from."

Roane's eyes widened perceptibly, and Wint began to swear. "Damnation, now didn't I tell you I had me one smart young'un here? If we was to send her to Washington, she'd have that whole palaverin' bunch o' politicians straightened out in no time.'' He beamed proudly, but Cleo was more interested in Roane's reaction.

Her eyes lingered on his mouth a moment too long. His lips were still moist with a trace of her brandied mincemeat pie, and before she could school her mind to proper rectitude, she imagined what it would be like to kiss away that sweetness.

"Name your price," he repeated firmly, meeting her eyes with dismaying directness.

Cleo's thoughts scattered under the searching look. It took a moment to round them up again. He *couldn't* have read her mind—the thought had whipped past in a split second. Steeling herself, she said, "I want your promise that Wint can stay right here for as long as he wants to." There, let him try to weasel out of that deal!

Holding the swaddled pie reverently, Roane said, "If you'll fulfill your part of the bargain, then Wint has a home on Gallagher land for as long as he wants it."

The words seemed to reverberate in the ensuing silence. Wint, his thin voice suspiciously unsteady, spoke first. Solemnly, he said, "I beswear if that ain't the nicest thing anybody's ever done fer me, boy. An' jest to show I don't take nothing fer granted, I'm goin' to shine this old dump up and make it a real showplace."

Cleo felt strangely shaken. She had been joking—or at least she thought she had. Somehow the whole thing seemed to have backfired on her, but if Wint had come out of it the winner, then that was what was important.

It had been a fluke, a spur of the moment gesture on her part, but the pie had evidently done the trick. Nollie sent word through Wint just before dark that if she'd care to come up to the house first thing in the morning, he'd show her how to use his range.

Wint popped open a can of beer as he passed on the message, and Cleo impulsively reached for another one. Solemnly, they toasted the capitulation of the Gallagher empire. "Gal, you used yer head that time," Wint declared proudly. "I don't mind tellin' you, I was plum tore up when you handed over my pun'kin pie, but when the boy come out with his pronouncement, why I dang near commenced bawling. Now, the next thing we got to do is to get you all squared away with a good man. You done your part—I'll do mine."

Grimacing at both the words and the taste—she kept forgetting that she didn't care for beer—Cleo shook her head in exasperation. "You do and I'll never speak to you again. Wint, why can't you get it through your head that I'm happy just the way I am?" She parked the nearly full can on the counter. "Look at me," she exclaimed, extending her arms as if she meant the words literally. "I'm all grown up now...my life belongs to me, and only me. I'm *free.* Don't you understand? I *like* my life. I like *me.* I don't *need* a husband hanging around my neck like an albatross. My ego isn't dependent on being Mrs. anybody. I have—"

"Aw right, aw right, hang it up," Wint muttered, snaffling her beer and tossing his empty can in the garbage. "I get the picture. You're one o' them liberated females I keep readin' about. Don't need *no*body. Well, let me tell you somethin', young'un, there's many a cold night ahead of you, and when you get to be my age, it's too late to do a dang thing about it. Ain't no woman would look at the likes o' me now, an' I'll tell you the truth—there's times when I'd give a heap to have some old battle-ax settin' across the table from me, her head full o' curlers and her lip full o' snuff. Instead, I got me a onery old he-goat to pick fights with an' a pen full o' roosters to squabble at me ever time I set foot out the door. That's as close to havin' me a wife as I can get."

Managing to keep her voice almost steady, Cleo shot back, "And what are the bees for? Honey or venom?"

Looking remarkably like one of his bantam roosters, Wint shook his head so that his blue-black hair waved stiffly. He snorted, "When it comes to honey, you could learn a thing or two, girl. A man's like a bee—he'll go where there's nectar to be found. You're a looker, all right—no two ways about it—but looks ain't ever'thing. You take them alfalfa blossoms—purty as a picture and ain't no honey any sweeter, but a bee, he'll go to most any other kind o' flower afore he'll stick his head into an alfalfa blossom.''

Cleo, feeling thoroughly chastened, sank meekly into a chair and waited for her impromptu lesson in beekeeping to end. Wint was not normally a garrulous man, but evidently what had happened a few hours before had broken the seal on his emotions.

''Y'see, the alfalfa blossom, she jest sets there, lookin' all sweet and fetchin', but as soon as a bee sets down on her, she'll spit her pollen out and hit him right smack dab between the eyes. A bee, he don't care for that. No-siree,'' the wizened little man declared earnestly. ''As sweet as that nectar is, an' as much as he'd like to whomp up a batch o' alfalfa honey, he'll go sum'mers where he's treated right. An' it ain't''—he shook a knotty finger in her face—''to no liberated female who spits her pollen between his eyes!''

The big wood stove came as close to intimidating her as anything had in a long time, but in the face of both Wint's and Nollie's encouragement, Cleo was determined to master the thing. After all, now that the walls of Jericho had come tumbling down, the least she could do was step inside.

"Now, once I get 'er banked down good, I open the door like this—" The old cook twisted the coiled handle, disdaining the use of a potholder. "I poke my hand inside about this far, and when it draws on my fingernails thisaway"—he took her hand before she could snatch it away and held it just inside the cavernous oven, and Cleo felt the odd drawing sensation under her nails—"it's jest right fer biscuits. You want to cool 'er down some fer cakes and pies and turkeys."

There was more. The kitchen had been built to cook for an army, and as he showed her the pantry, with its huge bins that had once held flour, meal and sugar and the mammoth freezer, which was the most modern piece of equipment in sight, Nollie regaled her with stories of harvest crews putting away whole steers in a single meal. "I could cook me up a storm in them days," the cook confided sadly. "To tell the truth, there ain't no satisfaction in cookin' no more."

So where was the big conflict? Cleo wondered later as she sat alone in the kitchen

working up a shopping list. Wint and Nollie
had gone out with their heads together half
an hour before, and she had no idea when or
if they'd be back. Nollie had caved in without a whimper, and Wint was assured of his
home, which meant she could go home with
the satisfaction of a job well done.

A door slammed, and Roane came in
chafing his hands together. His face was
reddened from the cold wind that was blowing in from the northwest, but he was grinning broadly. "How's it going?" he inquired
genially, coming to stand behind her.

His cold knuckles burrowed into the warm
hollow of her neck, and she shrieked. Before she could escape, he was leaning over
her, reading the long list she had prepared.
"Tell you what," he said. "I can help you
locate all this stuff if you don't mind riding
in the truck. Pete drove the car to the airport, so he can haul our company back after he collects them. They'll probably be here
about dark, but we'd still have time to shop
and grab a bite of lunch if you want to."

She turned to face him, the maneuver deliberately designed to put some space between them. "In the first place, Nollie might

be planning to do the shopping, and I'd hate to overstep my authority. In the second place, they're not 'our' company; they're *your* company. And in the third place—"

Grinning broadly, Roane slipped a hand under each of her arms and lifted her off the chair. "And in the third place, honey, forget the first two places," he ordered. "Nollie hates to shop, you couldn't overstep your authority if you tried, and it's *our* company—not mine."

Her lips parted to rebut his rebuttal, and he closed them with swift efficiency. Cleo's small whimper of exasperation went unnoticed as Roane warmed to his task, his arms going around her to lift her against him. Her arms instinctively found their way beneath his heavy jacket, and her hands latched onto a handful of warm flannel shirt.

It wasn't fair. It really wasn't fair for a man to have all the advantages Roane had. She had to fight like crazy to keep from going under every time she even looked at the man, and then he had to go and kiss her when he knew damned well she couldn't resist him.

At first, his tongue only teased her, luring her out to play, but all too quickly the kiss changed into something quite different. The playful caress turned into a game of another sort, and Cleo's mind registered every nuance of that change—in the way he held her, the way his body responded to her nearness. When he groaned a muffled invitation against her throat, it was all she could do not to lead the way.

"Come upstairs and let's check out those bedrooms," he urged hoarsely. His hand had slipped under her sweater, and his fingers burrowed underneath her bra. The fingers were warmer by now, but his touch was every bit as electrifying as those cold knuckles against her neck had been.

No. Oh, not again, she wailed inwardly. Desperately, she tried to convince herself that he was only teasing her, that they weren't really in danger of repeating yesterday's mistake, but how could she trust him? Around temptation of this caliber, she couldn't even trust herself.

Roane's breath was as ragged as hers, his heartbeat as accelerated, and he brushed his open mouth back and forth over hers in a tantalizing way while his large, hard hands moved down to spread over her hips. Cupping and lifting, they held her in stunning proximity to his aroused body, and she moved instinctively against him.

It had to stop. This was crazy! Was she going to react this way every time a man held her in his arms from now on? To think she'd looked with contempt on women who couldn't get along without a man. At this rate, she'd be afraid even to shake hands with one again.

But she knew it wasn't just any man. It was Roane. Once exposed to him, she'd always be susceptible, and she'd been thoroughly exposed, she acknowledged hopelessly. She had the dubious satisfaction of knowing that it wasn't exactly one-sided. They were entirely too responsive to each other. The chemical reaction between them was just too volatile to be trusted. She rationalized madly, but it didn't help matters when his hungry mouth began caressing her eyelashes and moved to warm the tip of her nose before proceeding to her lips again.

"Roane, stop that," she implored. He had unfastened her bra, and now he was touching the tips of her sensitized breasts as if he were sending out code—which he was. She read the message loud and clear, and well he knew it.

"I don't want to stop it, Cleo," he murmured against her mouth.

"This is no place—"

"I know. Let's go upstairs."

She ducked under his arm and turned to glare at him in helpless frustration. A little while before, she had been congratulating herself on a job well done. Wonder Woman had swooped in from the East and solved the problem of Wint's security and Nollie's stranglehold on the kitchen with a single wave of her magic pie. The executive mind at work.

Now look at her! One glance from a pair of honey-colored eyes, one touch of a hand, one kiss, and she was ready to fall apart. Every bit of common sense she possessed simply flew out the window.

"Roane, for the last time, no! I don't want to go upstairs with you. I don't want to go anywhere with you. I don't want you to kiss me, and I—"

"The hell you don't," he growled. "You weren't exactly fighting me off just now, and for the record, where was all that maidenly reluctance yesterday? Am I imagining things, or did you take off your clothes and lie back in the—"

"Stop it!" Turning away, she covered her eyes with her palms. "Just shut up and let me alone," she grated. He made it sound as if—as if she had thrown herself at him, and it hadn't been that way. It hadn't been that way at all!

"Look," she pointed out, her firm jaw emphasizing her determination. "Yesterday was no one's fault. It just…happened. I told you it wouldn't happen again, and I meant exactly that. Roane, I'm not in the habit of sleeping with a man I've just met, and I don't intend to cultivate the habit. It has nothing to do with you or even with whether or not I enjoyed yesterday." She'd have preferred to crawl under the table and hide, but she managed to hold his eyes without flinching.

"You did," he said flatly. "You weren't faking, and I sure as hell wasn't."

"That has absolutely nothing to do with the matter. I don't deny that it was good. It was ... special," she admitted reluctantly. Just how special, he'd never know. She faced him squarely. "I'll be perfectly honest with you. I wouldn't have missed it for anything, Roane—the sunshine, the wind, the hawk. It was a very beautiful experience for me, and I'll always remember it, but it's over and done with, and I don't want to cheapen it by trying to repeat it."

He wouldn't let her go. Still in his coat, with his booted feet braced apart on the battleship-gray linoleum, he held her there by the sheer force of his personality. It was almost as if he were daring her to go one step further with her confession, to examine the real reason she was afraid to continue whatever it was they had started.

Silently, she pleaded with him to release her from the uncanny power of his golden eagle eyes. He turned away as if he heard her wordless plea. Removing his jacket, he hung it on the back of a chair, deliberately taking the time to smooth down the sheepskin collar. When he turned, it was to shatter her tenuous composure with a questioning look.

Damn it, why hadn't she escaped while she
had the chance? He'd let her off the hook,
and here she was, still fluttering around the
bait. She didn't have the brains of a gold-
fish.

"I'd like to think we could be friends,
Cleo."

Friends? Did he have any conception of
what he was asking? "I suppose we are," she
conceded cautiously.

"Then, as one friend to another, do you
think you could manage to be ready to go to
town in half an hour? I reckon we really
ought to be here when Pete gets back with
our house guests. Have you looked at the
rooms upstairs yet? Do you have something
in mind for supper, or is that still Nol's de-
partment?"

"Nollie and I have worked things out.
Don't worry. We won't disgrace you before
your house guests. As for the rooms, I
haven't had time to do anything upstairs. We
can shop first, and I'll tackle them later, or
if you have something better to do now, we
can put off the trip until after lunch. Suit
yourself—I just work here." She enjoyed the
last crack; she really did. She enjoyed

Roane's quick flash of annoyance even more.

"Cleo," he drawled warningly, and she backed away. "We're operating on a gentleman's agreement. If you want to risk turning it into something else, then you'd better be prepared to take the consequences."

Excitement kindled in her as she watched the narrowing of his pale gold eyes. Recklessness had never been a noticeable part of her makeup before. Maybe she'd been missing something all these years. Maybe she'd gotten addicted to the taste of power when she'd issued that ultimatum to Rand Smith. Look at what had happened as a result of that morning's work.

"If it's all the same to you, then," Roane said evenly, "we'll go in about half an hour. I've got a few phone calls to make first, and I'll pick you up at the trailer on the way out. There's a front coming in—"

"You mean a weather front? I thought it had gone through already. We went from the Bahamas to the North Pole in a matter of hours."

When would she learn to leave well enough alone? Reading Roane's eyes with unerring accuracy, Cleo knew he was thinking about the same thing she was. If she'd wandered out to the ravine that day, and he'd found her there, the story would have had a very different ending.

"So—we're in for another change," he observed quietly. "The panhandle's noted for them. What do you bet we have another balmy spell within a week?"

Cleo tilted her head in an unconsciously challenging manner. "Since I won't be here to find out, I'd better pass on that one."

Seven

It was amazing how much pleasure could be
found in driving around a strange town in a
muddy pickup truck and shopping for an
assortment of mundane items. If Cleo had
expected Roane to try and take advantage of
the situation, she needn't have worried.
Long before they reached the outskirts of
Guymon, any slight tension in the atmo-
sphere inside the well-appointed cab of
Roane's four by four had dissipated.

Stretching her long, jean-clad legs out to
take advantage of the heavy-duty heater, she

began to interrogate him about everything concerning the panhandle region and its sparse population. By the time they pulled into the parking lot of the town's largest supermarket, she had learned all about the little green bugs that attacked wheat and the little green bugs that attacked grain sorghum. She could laugh about the world's first cow-chip-throwing contest and frown at the risks of an early-peaking market when a grower was forced to graze out winter wheat or small grains through the spring.

"There's a lot of high-stakes gambling out here," Roane observed as he helped her slither out of the high cab, "but I guess there are risks in everything."

"I couldn't agree with you more," Cleo muttered under her breath. She moved away from his supporting hands the moment her feet touched the wet pavement.

The feminine surveillance that followed Roane's progress through the aisles of the supermarket was amusing, but then, any perennial bachelor with Roane's looks, not to mention his other assets, would be the subject of a few fantasies. *The line forms to the left, ladies. Please have your applica-*

tions ready. Come to think of it, for the sort of wife he had in mind, this was probably the logical place to start shopping. Shrugging, Cleo set about the business of forgetting what she couldn't change and enjoying what she had.

Roane teased her while she poked and prodded every turkey in the cooler before selecting the one she wanted. She jeered at his insistence on stocking up on mincemeat and coconut and then making a special trip to buy several bottles of a moderately priced brandy.

"If you're suddenly stricken with a blinding urge to bake more mincemeat pies, I don't want to stand in your way," he drawled. "On the other hand, I don't necessarily want you raiding my private stock of Eau de Vie de Poire."

"Well, la de da de *da*!" Cleo caroled facetiously. "I didn't know cowboys went in for French brandy."

Before she could dance out of reach, he caught her by the back of her collar and gave it a hard yank. "Well, la de da de *da,*" he mocked. "That's lesson number two for you, isn't it?"

One look at the wicked quirk of his brow, and she subsided meekly. She wouldn't touch that one with a ten-foot pole.

After loading half the back of the truck with groceries, Roane slammed the camper shut, and they tackled the next item on the list. In her one quick dash upstairs, Cleo had noted the absence of any form of window covering in the bedrooms. Dust catchers, Nollie had called them derisively. He had long since disposed of them, and Cleo could only imagine that Roane's past house guests had been forced to hang a bedspread over the tall, bare windows if they valued privacy.

Under the circumstances, window shades were the best she could do. "They'll protect your girlfriends' modesty," she observed on the way out of the variety store, "but they won't do much to relieve the grimness of all that heavy mission oak furniture."

"If you've got any ideas, speak up." He loaded the unwieldy parcel of shades into the back of the truck and turned to her for further orders. "I'm yours to command."

"I wouldn't want to put it to the test," she said dryly. "But at short notice, about all I can think of that might help is flowers—at least for your girlfriends' rooms." And then, in a guileless afterthought, she added, "Or will you be doubling up? Maybe we'd better concentrate on your room and forget the rest."

He turned down one of the town's handsome brick streets. "Better stick to the original plans, honey. I'm not opposed to doubling up, but I draw the line at tripling." Taking advantage of a red light, he shot her a wicked grin, and Cleo curled her fists tightly against the overwhelming desire to shove his grin back where it came from.

"Flowers," he mused. "Let's see. I seem to remember that Danni always prefers roses—dark red ones with stems half a mile long and no thorns, please. Marsha's strictly a green orchid type."

Cleo had a fleeting memory of Doug presenting her with twenty-one long-stemmed red roses. She decided arbitrarily that she wasn't going to like Danni. "Actually, I was thinking in terms of something a little more suitable for a dresser or a bedside table," she snapped. "I'd consider bachelor buttons, or maybe a Venus flytrap, but of course, you know best.'' She wasn't all that certain that she was going to like a green orchid type, either, come to think of it.

The florist's shop was warm and steamy, and the two women who worked there took one look at Roane's tall, powerfully constructed figure, clad in jeans, boots and a sheepskin vest, and started fluttering. Cleo deliberately turned away to wander about the long, narrow room, pretending a fascination with a display of dish gardens adorned with everything from match-stick drilling rigs to tiny plastic cattle. She refused point-blank to enter into the discussion up at the front counter, and Roane was left in the eager hands of the two pink-smocked women, who were obviously only too willing to drag out every blossom in the cooler for his approval.

Guymon was *his* town. Marsha, Danni and Hal Wayland were *his* guests. *He* knew how much he wanted to spend on them and what sort of thing they'd be apt to enjoy. Personally, she'd prefer a bouquet of broom straw to the blue and lime-green carnations the simpering blonde was poking under his nose, but then there was no accounting for tastes.

At least he had the good sense to reject the ghastly dyed blossoms, but when she heard him attempting to explain what he meant by bedroom flowers, she was forced to hide her face in an enormous spray of eucalyptus. A small gasp of laughter escaped her, and Roane shot her an accusing look, and from then on, business was conducted in hushed tones. Finally, Roane took out his check-book, and Cleo wandered up to the front of the shop in time to hear him promise to collect his purchases after lunch.

"If I have to pick out the flowers single-handed, then I get to pick out a restaurant," he informed her, pulling away from the curb and making a U turn in the middle of the block.

"Single-handed! It looked to me like you had all the help you could use. The blonde might even be worth running through the squeeze. She looked like the type who could handle Nollie with one hand tied behind her."

Roane's derisive glance spoke volumes. "Let's look over my first two candidates before you start cutting any more out of the herd," he said dryly. "How do you like Mexican food?"

"A lot better than I like green orchids," she shot back impulsively. She loved Mexican food—what she'd had of it. So why couldn't she have said so without wrapping it around a snide comment about his girlfriend's taste in flowers? Anyone would think she was jealous.

The Mexican food she had sampled in North Carolina bore little resemblance to the assortment Roane ordered without bothering to consult her. "Why did you specify the red instead of the green sauce, and what's the difference? What if I'd preferred the green?" she demanded. She couldn't decide whether to be amused or irritated by his highhandedness. "Did it occur to you that I might have an opinion of my own?"

His attempted look of contrition wouldn't have fooled a hat rack. "But I thought you said you didn't care for green."

"I meant green orchids. What's that got to do with chilis? And stop looking like a tomcat with a mouth full of feathers!" Oh, for Pete's sake, couldn't she even get her foot out of her mouth long enough to eat lunch?

The food was hot in all respects and perfectly delicious. Cleo, promising herself not to utter one more word about Roane's girlfriends and their floral preferences, devoured it eagerly. Halfway through, she asked for the menu again so that Roane could interpret it for her. Then, over a delectable caramel-topped flan, she surveyed the few other diners. It was after two, and the lunch-time rush was long past.

"Oklahoma Mex is a little different from Carolina Mex," she observed, sipping on her third glass of ice water. "But you know something? I'll bet we'd have just as many blue jeans, curly brimmed hats and cowboy boots in the CW Bar Café in Burlington on any given Saturday night."

"Could be, but how many of those jeans would show saddle wear on the seat, and how many boots have stepped in—"

"You win!" she said, laughing. "But tell me this—what part of the saddle makes those little circular patches on the hip pocket? Or is that some exotic designer label I've missed?"

He swung around in his seat, resting a long arm across the back of the booth as he surveyed the three men who sauntered out. They were picking their teeth, and all three wore identical faded jeans, high-heeled boots and broad-brimmed hats. Two of them had the circular worn places on their hips that she'd noticed on both Rado and Josie, as well as half the men in town.

"Is that what you mean?"

She nodded. If Roane's jeans had shown similar wear, she'd have seen it long before now. Her eyes had spent more time dwelling on those taut, muscular buttocks than she cared to admit.

His gaze narrowed lazily as he turned his attention back to her, and the crooked smile that lifted the corners of his mouth was rife with speculation. "What's it worth to you?"

"About three cents, tops."

"How come you noticed something like that?" he asked curiously, and she lifted her eyes to his ruggedly defined hairline and wondered if chili peppers could affect a woman's judgment. She wasn't about to admit that she'd noticed because she'd been automatically comparing other men's physiques with his, to their decided disadvantage.

"Forget it."

"I'm curious," he persisted. The golden glint in his eyes was steadily undermining the remnants of her composure.

"Look, my business just happens to be people," she explained a little desperately. "I use all sorts of criteria in summing them up."

"Including what they carry in their hip pockets? Do you make a man turn out his pockets on your desk before you'll consider hiring him? Take a guess, then. What would a feed-lot hand be likely to haul around in his hip pocket?"

The whole thing had gotten completely out of hand. She'd only been trying to steer the subject away from his girlfriends! "They're probably saddle blisters. How did we get off on this business, anyway?" she exclaimed. "Let's get back to the ranch. I've got two days' work to do this afternoon, and for all I know, Wint and Nollie are gone for the day."

"Texhoma again?"

"They didn't bother to announce their plans," she grumbled. It suddenly occurred to her that whether or not Nollie saw fit to help out, she was going to have her work cut out for her getting three guest rooms ready and cooking meals for a business partner and a couple of females who'd probably be too busy draping themselves all over Roane to notice what they ate. "Let's get out of here."

The short walk through the bracing cold wind to where they had left the truck did a lot to restore Cleo's good mood. By the time Roane handed her up into the cab, she was teasing him again to tell her what made the distinctive mark on the seats of so many pairs of jeans.

He backed around and pulled out onto the street, heading for the highway that quickly carried them out of town. "Are you going to tell me?" she repeated.

"What'll you give me if I do?"

"An extra serving of mincemeat pie tomorrow." She hooked a knee on the seat and watched the playful expression on his strong features. It was a childish game, but she couldn't resist it.

"Not good enough. I intend to claim that, anyway."

"Over my dead body," she crowed with a pretense of indignation.

"I've got better uses for your body than eatin' pie from it, but if you insist."

"Maybe I'll let Nollie make dessert," she mused. Her pulses had taken a sharp jolt as her visual imagination flashed out a tantalizing picture, and she kept her gaze studiously focused on the mile after mile of tumbleweed-lined fences they passed.

"Sounds enticing, doesn't it?" Roane murmured after several minutes had passed.

"What does?"

"Your naked body plastered with mincemeat pie and me without so much as a fork to help me clean it up."

"Roane—" She attempted to force her lips into a forbidding line, but it was a lost cause. "Keep your mind on your driving, will you? I'd like to think those eggs in the back won't be scrambled by the time we get home."

They reached the state road that marked the northeast corner of the Gallagher ranch, and Roane slowed down. "It's tobacco," he said. "The chewing variety. It comes in a flat, round can."

Suspicious of his easy capitulation, Cleo nodded slowly. "Thanks. I was going to ask Josie or Rado."

"I figured you were. That's why I thought I'd better tell you first. Can't have them trying to claim my reward." The truck had slowed almost to a stop, and he pulled over to the shoulder of the road and set the parking brake.

"What's the matter?"

"Nothing's the matter. I just thought we'd wind this business up before we get involved up at the house."

Cautiously, she began edging farther into her corner. "Wind up what business?"

"Now come on, honey. If I can remember how these games used to be played back in my school days, then I'm damned sure you haven't forgotten. After all, you started it."

He reached for her, and she shook off his hand. "Roane, have you lost your feeble mind? I don't have the slightest idea what you're talking about." Of course she did. She'd been playing games with him all day— teasing, taunting games that skated around the edges of the real issue.

"Then I'll refresh your memory," he offered in a deep, purring drawl. "The game starts when the party of the first part—that's you—throws out the initial challenge. Then the party of the second part—that's me—picks it up, and the game is on. It begins to get interesting when the winner says, 'Pay off,' and the loser says, 'I won't.' Then he says, 'You will,' and she says, 'Make me.'" A slow, feral smile spread over his face. "And he does."

Cleo felt behind her for the door handle as he began to close the distance between them. She could have kicked herself when he slipped an arm behind her back and dragged her from her corner. Hadn't she sworn to walk away from Roane Gallagher and not look back? So how come every move she made, every word she said, was deliberately designed to taunt him into retaliation? Had she always been this reckless, or was it only the catalytic effect Roane had on her senses?

Roane savored the feel of her beneath his hungry hands. She smelled like rain, and she tasted like brown sugar, and if he thought he could get away with it, he'd haul her back into the camper and make love to her on top of the eggs, the turkey and six boxes of flowers! She'd been deliberately playing with him all day, and when she wasn't doing it deliberately, she was even more tantalizing. Hanging over the meat cooler in the grocery store with that delectable rump of hers just begging for a swat—it had been all he could do to keep his hands off her.

He applied a more insistent pressure, and her lips parted sweetly. She was attracted to him; he knew she was. She was basically too honest to try and deny it, so why this backing off every time he tried to get close to her? Whatever this thing between them was, it was too damned potent to ignore.

She wouldn't give him her tongue, and he went after it. She didn't struggle. On the other hand, she wasn't letting herself go, either.

That damned—he thrust his tongue aggressively into her mouth and slipped his hands down to her hips—*stubborn chin of hers!* He found the waistband of her jeans and ran his hand down inside, savoring the cool satin feel of her hips. *Resist me, will you?* She tried to squirm away from his hands, and he let his fingers bite into her firm flesh. *I know exactly how to set fire to you, woman, and we both know it.*

Cleo shuddered with the strain of holding back. She couldn't win when it came to a show of brute strength, but she refused to give him the satisfaction of a response. Her lips had opened to him instinctively before she'd had time to marshal her defenses, and he'd been quick to pounce.

Well, we'd see how he liked having an iceberg in his arms. As long as she kept her mind on something else, as long as she could hold out against the agonizing compulsion to crawl all over him, she'd be safe.

Chicken and string beans and coleslaw, she reiterated desperately. His hand had moved out of her jeans, and he was fumbling with the hook on her bra. An eighteen wheeler roared by with a deafening blast of the horn, and Roane didn't even have the grace to pause. *Biscuits and gravy, and sillabub for dessert.* His fingers moved under her breast and slipped up to find the evidence he was seeking in her taut, swollen nipples.

Damn! Three in the afternoon, in the cab of a truck beside a public highway, and it was all she could do to keep from peeling the clothes right off his body! She could recite a week's menus and a whole blasted cookbook, and it wouldn't help—not when he was tantalizing her to the point of insanity with his hands and his mouth and his body.

"Had enough?" he whispered hoarsely into her ear. He eased her position on his lap, groaning when she brushed across the blatant evidence of his own turmoil. "I can't say I think much of my own judgment. It's been a long time since I pulled anything quite this stupid." His voice was raw, and his hands, when he lifted her back onto the seat beside him, unsteady.

Cleo managed a painful parody of a smile. "If you're looking for an argument on the subject, forget it. How about dropping me off at Wint's?"

She answered his protest by saying she needed to feed the livestock in case Wint wasn't back yet. But before she fed anything, she promised herself silently, she intended to have herself a long, cold shower. "If you don't want to bother with putting away the groceries, just leave them out on the kitchen table. Nothing's going to thaw out very quickly in that house.''

''Nothing except you,'' he retorted, switching on the engine and idling slowly as far as the main gate.

Her toes curled inside her short suede boots, and she jutted her chin resolutely. ''Don't hold your breath.''

Poised at the foot of the steps, Cleo juggled the three containers she'd found for the flowers and listened to the murmur of voices coming from the living room. Pete Myers, Roane's foreman and pilot, had delivered the two women half an hour before, and he'd stayed for a drink before going home to his wife and family. Now there were only the four of them in there. Cleo had met Pete when she'd met the others—Hal Wayland, Roane's partner, who had driven from Tulsa, Marsha Ikert, a sultry brunette who claimed to be a decorator, and the effervescent little Danni Meekum, who didn't claim to be anything.

The sudden increase in volume signified the opening of a door, and rather than be caught lurking on the stairway, Cleo took the stairs two at a time. She had managed to cook the chicken without scorching it, and it was on the warming shelf above the range while the oven heated—she hoped—sufficiently to brown the biscuits. She'd given up on the string beans after staring helplessly for five minutes at the neat stack of firewood and trying to figure out how many chunks it took to go from chicken temperature to buttermilk biscuits.

The bedrooms were frigid, and there wasn't anything she could do about it. Somewhere in this drafty old barn, there was a furnace, but you couldn't prove it by her. Wint had told her that old Dave had been stubborn and thrifty, but this was ridiculous! The furniture must have been bought when the house was new. Except for the master bedroom, which she hadn't seen yet, and the room Roane had used as a boy, none of it had been changed since Mrs. Gallagher had died.

Moving quickly in deference to the damp coldness, Cleo arranged the assortment of cut flowers Roane had bought and put a generous arrangement in each of the two women's rooms. If anything, they only added to the bleakness of the cold white walls, the bare floors and the ungainly furniture. She hurried to the room where Hal was to sleep and left the remaining flowers on the chest of drawers. It would have to do. She'd ransomed her Thanksgiving holiday in exchange for Wint's security, but she hadn't promised any miracles.

Dashing downstairs again, she entered the kitchen by one door in time to see the other one swing closed. It wouldn't have been Wint or Nollie—they'd brought in a supply of stove wood and then announced their plans to go visit a friend in Texhoma, leaving her with the whole show to produce. She'd been torn between exasperation and relief, but the exasperation had outlasted the relief after the sixth trip upstairs to see to the needs of the house guests.

Dammit, Roane could have at least offered to hang the blasted window shades! They were still propped on the landing where she'd left them three hours ago, and at this rate they wouldn't get hung at all.

The meal was ready, and Cleo stuck her head through the door to announce it. She'd been tempted to use Nollie's methods but didn't quite have the nerve. Unless she

missed her bet, she was in for a round or two
with Roane before she got out of there, anyway, and there was no point in riling him up
beforehand.

He nodded to the centerpiece. "That arrangement was meant for you," he said
softly when she brought in the fricassee and
placed it at the head of the table. She'd
opened the largest box from the florist to
discover a lavish assortment of potted cacti.
The card had read simply, "Cleo." Most of
the plants were ready to burst into bloom,
and she wouldn't even hazard a guess as to
whether or not that fact held any signifi-
cance. After locating a yellowed cutwork
cloth, she had taken great satisfaction in
placing the low, round bowl in the center of
the dining-room table.

"Thank you, Roane—they're lovely," she
said sweetly, removing the lid from the
chicken. "But then you're an expert in
choosing suitable flowers for all your
friends, aren't you?"

The three others filed in, and Roane
seated Cleo and then the others, and then he
took his place at the head of the table. Cleo
was still wearing her jeans—there hadn't

been time to run back to the trailer and change, and she wasn't about to tackle that tree-eating monster in the kitchen in white silk pants and a velvet pullover. Hal Wayland, an attractive man in his late forties with a quiet manner and the eyes of a sharpshooter, wore informal western attire, as did Roane.

As for the two women, Cleo hadn't quite decided what to think of them. Her initial reaction had been positive toward the bubbly little redhead from Tulsa and negative toward the cool-eyed sophisticate from Oklahoma City.

Marsha's manners were flawless, and her reaction to Cleo's presence had been pleasant enough on the surface, but Cleo had withheld judgment. The stakes were too high for any contender to dismiss the competition, and even if Cleo was no competition, Marsha was definitely a contender. That much had been obvious from the first. That night she was dressed with a casual, understated elegance that was perfect for the situation. Cleo awarded her five points for dressing to the occasion.

On the other hand, Danni, younger than either of the other two women by several years, had floated downstairs in a full-length brocade and lace outfit that would have been more effective without the goose bumps. Roane had been the one to fetch her a shawl and spread it solicitously over her bare shoulders while he apologized again for the inefficient heating system.

How did one score that performance, Cleo wondered as she passed Hal a second serving of her special dill and sour cream coleslaw. No marks at all for clothes sense. Still, one couldn't dismiss the fact that that little Scarlett O'Hara get-up had drawn forth more reaction from Roane than had Marsha's three hundred dollars' worth of flea-market chic.

All in all, the game promised to be most entertaining, Cleo assured herself. She allowed her gaze to dwell for a moment on the instigator of the whole charade, and then she viciously forked into the succulent chicken on her plate.

Eight

It was hard to put her finger on the precise moment when the game ceased to be amusing. Hal was a comfortable guest, equally charming to each of the women, and Marsha and Danni seemed to take in stride having the niece of the Gallagher beekeeper and blacksmith cook dinner and then take her place at the table in her jeans. No one seemed to stand on ceremony, and the mood of the evening was generally relaxed and congenial.

DIXIE BROWNING   183

The food disappeared readily enough. For
someone of Marsha's fashion-model pro-
portions, she accounted for a surprising
amount of it, and Hal was lavish with his
compliments as he helped himself to the last
biscuit. The only thing left when the two
couples filed out of the dining room was half
a serving of slaw and a couple of chunks of
the watermelon pickles she had picked up at
the market.

Impatiently, Cleo brushed away Roane's
offer of assistance. She began to stack the
dishes beside the sink, her stride growing
brisker with every trip through the swinging
doors. By the time she had transferred the
lot, she had made up her mind that she was
not going to spend the next hour over a sink
filled with dirty dishes. Indulging herself in
an orgy of righteous indignation, she was
busy composing her declaration of independence when the door swung open and
Roane strolled in.

"Honey, you're not going to wash those
things. I forgot to mention it, but Rado's
boy's coming in at the crack of dawn to
clean up. He's helped out in a pinch before—picks up a little extra on the side that
way."

Suddenly deflated, Cleo actually caught herself on the verge of arguing with him. She felt an instinctive need to be angry, and Roane had no business cheating her out of a just cause.

"I'm not going to cook breakfast," she warned him, furiously scraping the last of the slaw into a plastic bag for Wint's chickens.

"Of course you're not going to cook breakfast, honey." His tone was insufferably reasonable, clearly meant to be soothing, and she hotly resented it.

Dammit, she didn't need to be soothed! She glared at him sullenly, knowing she was being childish and unable to do anything about it. "I just thought you ought to know," she muttered.

"I've got two perfectly able-bodied women in the house. Between them, they ought to be able to come up with something to last us until you get that turkey cooked."

Of all the chauvinistic remarks! It wouldn't occur to him to fry his own damned egg! "I'll take your word for just how able-bodied they are," she snapped, and when the unintentional double meaning struck her, she turned away and began fumbling with the pile of used flatware. Something was definitely wrong with her. Not even Rand Smith at his most infuriating had affected her as much. "These need washing tonight," she grumbled.

"Honey, what's the matter? Are you tired? Look, leave that stuff—I don't care about that."

The concern in his voice sounded genuine, but illogically, it only enraged her more. "Well, you certainly should. It's obviously heirloom silver—it would cost a fortune today!"

"I reckon I could manage to produce a fortune quicker than I could produce an heir. I'll risk a little tarnish," he teased gently. "Now get your mitts out of that dishwater and stop acting up, honey." His hands came down on her shoulders and then slid to her elbows, and he pulled her resisting body back against him. "What's bothering you, Cleo?" His mouth was against the back of her head, and she could feel his breath stirring in her hair. "Has our little joke gone far enough? Do you want to call it off?"

"Joke?" A streak of deep-seated contrariness refused to be placated so easily. "What joke? We struck a bargain—I cater your house party, and you give Wint a lifetime right to his homesite. You're not going to back out now."

His fingers bit deeper into the flesh of her arms, and he turned her around to face him. His narrowed eyes bored relentlessly into hers "I seem to recall there was something more to it than that," he drawled. "You refused my proposal of marriage. Instead, you offered to put up your professional services against Wint's half acre. The extras you threw in were just to sweeten the pot."

"Oh, knock it off, Roane. We both know just how serious you were about finding yourself a wife. You deliberately exaggerated the thing with Nollie—you and Wint both. I don't see Nollie crying in his beer because someone else took over his kitchen tonight," she jeered.

"Your expert handling," he told her gravely. "Honest. It never would have occurred to me to go after him with a pumpkin pie and hope he'd take the bait."

Was he really serious? No—he couldn't be. Frustrated, Cleo gritted her teeth impotently. It was impossible to meet his eyes. It was equally impossible to look elsewhere. He was the most compelling man she had ever met, and the more he compelled, the more nervous she grew. The nervousness transmuted itself into anger, and she blazed out at him. "Look, you want my expert advice? I'll give it to you! Lease the ranch to someone with a cast-iron stomach and go back to Tulsa. Buy yourself a condo, hire a housekeeper and start swinging again, because frankly, if you're hunting for a wife, and those two in there are your top contenders, you're fresh out of luck. I don't think either of them would last out six weeks."

"You're tired," Roane murmured gently.

"Damn it, I am not tired. Stop patronizing me! You asked my opinion—you got it. What more do you want?" She was ranting like a shrew, and she couldn't seem to stop it, and if he didn't let go of her so that she could get out of there, she was going to hit him!

"You know what I want, Cleo. Don't you?" His voice was a silken purr that awakened some atavistic element deep inside her. "I'll tell what I really want. I want to take you upstairs and lay you down on my bed and very slowly remove every stitch of your clothes. Then I want you to undress me. And do you know what I want after that?"

Her mouth had dropped open, and when she realized it, she snapped it shut like a steel trap. "I can tell you what you'd get," she jeered. "Pneumonia!"

He threw back his head and roared, and in spite of herself, Cleo began to thaw. Her chin quivered, and then the grim line of her lips broke apart, and she was laughing helplessly, leaning against Roane with her backside against the enormous porcelain sink.

Almost as soon as she became aware of the feel of his deep laughter against her body, Cleo became aware of other sensations. One set of muscles grew still as another set grew increasingly tense, and his husky voice made a question of her name.

"Cleo?"

Helplessly, she lifted her face to meet his eyes. His pupils had expanded to cover all but a ring of pale gold, and she parted her lips to meet him halfway.

It was like coming home. It was like Chinese food. A few hours ago, he had kissed her thoroughly in the truck beside the highway, and now she was starving for him again. Her wet, soapy hands clung to his shoulders, clutching the rock-hard muscles through a thin layer of silky cotton shirt. He was pressing her against the rim of the sink so that she was totally aware of his swiftly rising passion. Hot, sweet fire streaked through her loins as she moved against him instinctively.

"Honey, stop it—you're driving me loco," he groaned, rolling his head so that the side of his mouth was still in contact with hers. Great ragged breaths of air tore into his lungs.

Her fingers curled against the flat muscles of his sides. She *wanted* to drive him loco. She wanted to drive him so wild that he'd sweep her off her feet and make her forget all about freedom and independence and self-sufficiency.

"What time will you be here tomorrow morning? That's a pretty hefty turkey you're going to tackle." His voice was almost under control again, and he eased her away from the sink, one arm still holding her tightly.

Ice water quenched the fire that had threatened to rage out of control. She jerked herself from his embrace. Oh, good lord, what did it take to teach her the rudiments of survival?

Roane watched the swift change set in. That chin of hers was an unerring barometer. The higher it went, the closer the storm. "Honey, what did I do? What did I say?"

He watched her stalk across the room to snatch her coat from the rack. Her shoulders were ramrod stiff, and her hips . . .

A reluctant grin spread over his face; she was a sight to behold when she was mad. Like a stiff-legged colt. Like that sorrel mare he'd been working with until he'd gotten too busy with other things. Unfortunately, he suspected there was something more to her skittishness than met the eye. He wished to hell he could convince himself that the only reason she was upset was because he'd had to break it off that way. He shouldn't have started anything with the others in the next room—he'd only meant to gentle her down, but he'd overestimated his self-control.

Dammit, he'd had to do something! She affected him like wildfire—like one of the grass fires that could catch from a single spark and cover hundreds of acres before it was brought under control.

A shrill of laughter came from the living room. Danni. Roane's eyes were still on Cleo, and he saw her tighten up another notch. He'd like to think it was jealousy, but he wasn't that big a fool. She'd made it pretty clear from the first that she wasn't interested in any sort of a long-term affair, and ironically, he was beginning to wonder if he'd be satisfied with anything less.

"I'll be here by nine," she announced flatly.

"I'll drive you home."

"Don't bother. I have my car."

There was no sign of anger in her voice now, but he could have sworn she was still mad. She looked cool and disinterested, and it puzzled him. It did more than that. It got under his skin. His eyes narrowed, but he continued to lean casually against the counter.

"Good night, Roane."

He nodded. She didn't see it. She didn't bother to look at him, but he followed her progress through the window as she marched briskly across the back yard under the light and slid into her car. She had to back out and turn around, and she did it with the neat efficiency that was so typical of her. He was still standing there, staring thoughtfully out through the tall, bare window, when Danni found him.

"Hi! Whatcha doing, honey? I thought I'd better come rescue you." Her wide blue eyes were as beautiful as ever, and in those fancy duds, she looked like a china doll.

Roane's mind strayed back to a tall, lean figure in jeans and a rumpled white cotton safari shirt, and he frowned absently. "Just checking on tomorrow's plans."

"I hope Cleo's cooking again. I remember that old man you had when I came out here with Daddy—he was revolting!"

"He's still around," Roane murmured, ushering her out as he flipped off the light. "Cleo just offered to pitch in and help out."

"Well, sure. Why shouldn't she? Didn't you say her uncle works for you?"

"Her great-uncle. Wint Lawrence was a part of this spread before I was even born. He was a great friend of Dad's—a blacksmith. Matter of fact, he made the ceiling fixture in the living room."

"Oh," she uttered vaguely. "It's cute."

Cute. With a sardonic twist of his lips, Roane thought about the handsome wrought-iron fixture that was the one decent-looking thing in the room. He had watched Wint make it all those years ago, determined to learn everything the old man knew and grow up to become a blacksmith himself. He had been about six at the time and enormously impressed by a man who could bend iron to his will.

Entering the living room, he took in the couple who were seated on the couch, drinks in hand as they talked earnestly about a certain series of tax-free municipal bonds. Beside him, Danni bemoaned the fact that he didn't have a stereo, and he heard himself muttering a vague promise to look into the matter.

What the devil had he been thinking of when he'd rounded up this particular trio? He must have had something in mind when he'd made those calls, but damned if he could recall just what it was. Aside from Hal, whom he had seen just the week before, anyway, he hadn't given a thought to any of them in months.

Marsha stood with the swift grace that suddenly struck him as reptilian. She smiled at him. "Would you like a drink?" she inquired graciously, as if she were already the hostess.

Absentmindedly, Roane declined, and then he crossed to pour himself a double whiskey, missing the three pairs of lifted eyebrows. Tossing back half of the shot in one gulp, he waited for the women to be seated before dropping into his own chair. It took a surprising amount of effort to drag his attention back to the company at hand.

He gave it a try. "Still seeing that stock-broker, Marsha?"

Her dark head tilted provocatively. "Any objections?"

"I'd have to see his track record first. Investments, that is—not women." His grin came readily, almost as if he gave a damn whom she spent her nights with. They'd been pretty tight at one time. She'd come up from Oklahoma City to do the offices and the public rooms at the plant. Hal's idea. Hal had been to a few too many management seminars.

It hadn't lasted, though. Marsha Ikert was entirely too intense for his tastes. Whatever she did, she threw the sum total of her energies into it. For a while, it had been acquiring the title of Mrs. Roane Gallagher for herself. He'd short-circuited that by inviting her out for a visit a few weeks after he'd taken over there. Compared to what it had been like then, the place was a resort hotel now.

Danni made a play for Roane's attention. She was the daughter of one of his business associates, and she'd had a crush on him at one time. It had been poor judgment on his part to invite her, but he'd thought it wise to dilute Marsha by having another female along, and everyone else he'd called at short notice had had other plans. "Roane, when are you coming back to town again?" the vivacious little redhead asked. "There's a dance coming up at the Silver Dollar Club, and I haven't decided on who's going to take me yet."

"Honey, a man'd have to be crazy to risk getting trampled in the stampede if word got out that you weren't already hogtied for a dance." His gentle smile took the edge off the rejection, and he turned to Hal with a question about the plant.

The eleven o'clock news was on when Danni announced her rather sulky decision to go up to bed. "Don't forget. You promised me we could go riding while I'm here."

"First thing Friday, hmmm?" Roane smiled absently, the matter already forgotten.

Marsha and Hal turned their attention to the market news, and Roane wandered over to the front window to stare out into the darkness. He could just see the glow from Wint's yard light from there. He was still standing there, rocking slowly back and forth on his heels, when Marsha moved silently up beside him to hook an arm through his.

"What do you see out there?" she asked in a sultry murmur.

"Hmmmm?"

"Darling, seriously, when are you going to level this old relic and start over? I could recommend a terrific architect, and I'd design the interior for you at cost."

"Hmmmm?"

Irritation creeping in under her finishing-school accents, she sniffed. "Roane, why exactly did you invite us out here, anyway? Hal, I can understand, but why that silly little Meekum girl?"

"Didn't you ever hear of social obligations, honey?"

"Don't make me laugh," she scoffed. "You never gave a damn for what society thought of you, and you never will. That's one of the more attractive things about you, unfortunately. Every woman dreams of taming a wild one."

His grin was only slightly preoccupied. "A wild what, honey?"

Ruefully, she shook her flawlessly coiffed head. "That, I've never quite figured out. I'd be interested in knowing more about the Lawrence girl. Is she a part of your social reformation?"

"Maybe I'm a part of hers. Who knows?"

Sighing, Marsha turned away. "One more for the road, then, darling, and I'll toddle along up to my chilly boudoir. I don't suppose you're offering any personal services to make up for the deficiencies of your heating system, are you?"

From across the room, Hal broke in with an offer that was promptly rejected, and then Marsha helped herself to another drink when the men both declined.

Long after the other two guests had gone upstairs, Roane leaned against the window, staring out at the gray, moonlit landscape and wondering what had happened to make him behave in such an uncharacteristic manner. A few years ago—even a few months ago—he'd have been more than happy to warm her bed. Or the bed of any of a dozen other women he could name. Marsha was beautiful, intelligent, amusing and evidently still willing. Furthermore, she was on the spot.

Danni was another matter. He'd known her since her college days, seeing her often in her father's home before she moved to Tulsa and her own apartment. He'd been delegated to keep an informal eye on her the first few months, but he'd always been careful to avoid personal involvement. He didn't want to hurt the girl. Knowing her father and having watched her grow up put her on a different footing, and he sure as hell couldn't see himself saddled with her permanently. She reminded him too much of Chrissy. Come to think of it, so did Marsha, which was odd. They were totally different.

Take the way they reacted to men. He'd invited Hal out because the poor guy was at loose ends since his divorce—still gun-shy. He needed to ease back into the social flow. Marsha had met him at the plant, of course, but this was the first time they'd seen each other on a personal level. He might have known she'd cut right through to Hal's steel-trap mind and start raiding with both of her greedy little hands. Danni wasn't interested in the quality of any man's mind except when it was focused on her. She reacted to the surface charm by batting her eyelashes and collecting her due in compliments.

Cleo had done neither. She'd smiled and listened, made a few astute remarks about the effects of recession on social security and corporate benefit plans and then sat back and left the field to the other two.

Cleo. He turned away and took a cheroot from the humidor, absently stroking the sides before clipping the end. Lighting up, he blew a stream of fragrant smoke up to the ceiling, where it drifted like Spanish moss around the graceful iron fixture.

Damn it, he was going to have to do something about her, and fast. But what? He had a gut feeling she was getting ready to bolt, and he couldn't allow it to happen. Not now. Not yet. Not until he figured out why she had such a powerful effect on him—and the exact nature of that effect.

Walking with light-footed swiftness, he left the house and crossed the wide, barren yard to the garage.

Cleo had not been asleep. Wint was still out, and she'd gone to bed mainly to keep from having to answer his questions when he got in. She'd lain there in the darkness and allowed her thoughts to skitter restlessly over the surface of her mind. When they snagged momentarily on the problem of Rand and her stalemated job, she arbitrarily made a decision.

She'd do it. She'd make the move. What did she have to lose? An apartment that was already too cramped? A few friends? Reba and Debbie had already decided to move with the plant. The crafts center where she took occasional classes in weaving? Certainly South Carolina would have something to offer along those lines. If not, she'd take up stamp collecting or clogging. Or bird watching.

She waited for the influx of satisfaction at having made her decision in such an unhurried, thoughtful manner. When it did come, she rolled over and planted her chin in her fists.

Whose bed was he in? Not Danni's. He was no cradle robber, whatever else he was. Marsha's? She'd watched Marsha's measuring glance take in everything in the house and dismiss it as hopeless. Everything except for Roane, that was.

A spray of something hard struck the window, and she reached behind her and tugged the blanket higher over the back of her neck. Trust a place like this to have tropical heat one day and sleet the next. It didn't occur to her that the moon had been bright enough to dim the stars when she'd left the house for the short drive home. She'd been in no mood to appreciate the beauty of a full moon.

It came again, and she flopped over and sat up. That wasn't sleet. It was gravel! Her feet hit the floor, and she winced at the gritty feel of the icy vinyl. "Dammit, Wint, it's about time—"

But it wasn't Wint's apologetic face that greeted her when she threw open the door. As soon as the breath rushed back into her lungs, she started flinging out questions. "Where is he? Has something happened to him? Have you come to tell me—"

"Whoa, honey—calm down, now. Take it easy."

The measured tones of Roane's drawling baritone convinced her that something awful had happened to Wint. "Roane, tell me," she whispered, allowing herself to be moved aside so that he could step inside and close the door.

She confronted him with her arms wrapped protectively around her pajama-clad body. "He's had an accident, hasn't he? I knew it. He's never been out this late before." She dropped into a chair and stared fixedly at the gleaming tan boots that were planted firmly on the floor in front of her.

"To the best of my knowledge," Roane declared judiciously, "Wint is in good health. That's not to say he's sober. You've been here just over a week now, and he's been on his best behavior, but your great-uncle, honey, is a man of parts. He has a social life, you know. There's a widow in Texhoma that he and Nollie have been courting for the past several years."

"Courting!" she squawked.

"Courting," he repeated. "But don't worry. Nothing's apt to come of it. They go at it as a team, chipping in to buy her flowers and candy, pairing up to escort her to whatever social events come up. I believe they're helping her install a new oil circulator tonight in exchange for an invitation to dinner tomorrow."

"Tomorrow," Cleo echoed dazedly, latching on to a word at random. "But that shouldn't take all night."

"What difference does it make? Honey, Wint's been his own keeper for about seventy years now."

Gingerly, she leaned back in her chair, her eyes still clinging distractedly to Roane's boots. Realization was slow in coming, and when it came, it swept over her like a cool, rising tide. Her gaze drifted up those long, muscular legs, braced apart in the lean whipcord pants. When it reached the small ornate buckle he wore, she frowned. "Then what are you doing here?"

Roane hitched up one of the chairs that matched the red Formica table and straddled it. "I'm not quite sure."

At that, she looked at him. Really looked at him. At the deep chest and the broad shoulders in the dark brown, western-cut shirt, at the powerful neck that was tanned from year-round outdoor activities, at the long, beautifully shaped head with the silky black hair and the eroded hairline, the long nose that had been broken at least once and the level shelf of a brow that shaded his clear, pale brown eyes. Last of all, she looked at his mouth, and that was her undoing. Jerking her eyes away from lips that could be both stern and sensuous at the same time, she caught sight of herself, huddled barefoot in the chair, wearing her pajamas and nothing else.

They were plain white, no-nonsense pajamas, but the fabric was one of the mills finest knits, and the resultant garment was both clinging and translucent. Her arms went around her body again, and she glared accusingly at the man across from her.

"What do you mean, you're not sure?"

Nine

"There's not a whole lot of room in these things, is there?" Roane mused, looking around him with every appearance of interest.

"There's enough."

"Do you ride?" He still wore that look of sincere interest, and Cleo narrowed her eyes as she studied him thoughtfully.

"Nothing fancy, but I manage to stay on." It occurred to her that he showed every evidence of being ill at ease, and the thought amused her. In fact, her own confidence soared in direct proportion to his growing discomfort. "Did you come to invite me to go for a moonlight ride?"

His grin lifted unevenly, revealing the chipped tooth. "I'm in the truck, but if the idea appeals . . . ?"

Without making a production of it, Cleo arranged her limbs for maximum protection against his marauding gaze. "I think I'll pass, thanks. What should I do about Wint's Thanksgiving dinner?"

"Why don't we leave him and Nollie in the capable hands of the Widow Potts? I've got a sneakin' suspicion that now they've gotten their two charges squared away, that pair's going to be hard to hold down."

Cleo stared absently at a box of fragrant honeycomb foundation while she struggled to sort out the latest development. "So much for Wint's semiannual deathbed letters," she muttered ruefully. At Roane's questioning look, she went on to explain how her great-uncle had shamed her into making the long trip. "One last time, he said. That wily old schemer; he led me to believe he was at death's door."

"But it worked," Roane said equably.

"What do you mean, it worked?"

"He has his security. Of course, he had it all along; only it hadn't been put into so many words." Standing up, Roane shoved the inadequate chair under the table and took a seat on the sofa. Several spools of Cleo's yarn rolled down the cushion to lodge against his thigh.

"Yes, well ... I appreciate it, Roane. I'm sure you wouldn't have thrown him out, anyway, but he was afraid that if you got married, your wife—"

"Which brings up another interesting matter," Roane put in, leaning back to extend an arm along the back of the sofa.

"Look, I don't know quite how we got off on this marriage kick, but don't you think the joke's wearing pretty thin by now? I mean, if you want to marry Danni or Marsha, that's your business, but—"

"But what?" There was nothing discernible in his manner to make her nervous. All the same, Cleo began to pinch tiny pleats in the hem of her pajama coat.

"But nothing. Oh, all right, then, if you insist on dragging out a bad joke, neither of them is exactly the sort I'd have picked to do your job for you. I don't think you really want a wife, Roane. A man doesn't get to be forty without—"

"Forty-one."

"What?"

"Sorry—I wouldn't want to mislead you into thinking you were getting a bargain. I'll be forty-one in a couple of months. I'm set in my ways, my hair's disappearing, I cuss too damn much, and I get airsick—which accounts for Pete's having to fly for me. On the other hand, I'm relatively solvent, I'm kind to women, children and animals, I drink and smoke only in moderation, and I'm told that I'm good in bed, all things considered."

Cleo's mouth hung open for several moments before she snapped it shut again. "Roane—" she blurted in startled, reluctant amusement, "I—"

"Yeah, I know," he said modestly. "But if I don't point out my good qualities, who will?"

She was dangerously close to crying. She was dangerously close to doing any number of wildly unsuitable things. She didn't know whether to laugh at him or bolt herself into the bedroom. She laughed.

"You find my proposal funny?" The plaintive note in his voice set her off even more.

"Proposal! Is that what it was?" she gasped.

"I'm not in the habit of issuing midnight testimonials without a good reason," he informed her indignantly, and she howled.

The more she laughed, the more impossible it became to stop, until finally, achieving a tearful semblance of sobriety, she gazed up into Roane's scowling face. He was leaning over her, a fist planted firmly on either side of her, and there wasn't a shadow of a smile in evidence.

"Are you quite finished?" he asked evenly.

"Roane, I'm sorry. I don't know what came over me. Honestly—I don't usually do things like this."

"You mean you don't make a habit of laughing in men's faces when they're trying to ask you to marry them?"

At that, she *really* sobered. "It's just a joke, Roane. Don't try to tell me your heart's broken—the guilt would ruin me."

"Do you know what you remind me of?"

Her voice still slightly unsteady, she said solemnly, "No. Unless it's a cactus. I got your rather pointed joke, you know. Ha ha. Pointed? Cactus?" Her eyes pleaded with him to laugh with her. At this hour of the night, it was far too easy to mistake a game for something more serious.

Roane bit off whatever he was planning to say and lifted her up by her arms, and this time there was no laughter, not even a mocking gleam in those golden eagle eyes. "Cleo—damn it, why won't you marry me? We're good together. At least we proved that much the other day out in the ravine."

Helplessly, she said, "Roane, I can't. I can't marry you, and I'm not going to have an affair with you, and that's that!"

"Can you at least tell me why?" The baffled note rang true, and Cleo knew she had to be honest with him. She cared too deeply for him to be otherwise. It was going to be like walking a tightrope, telling him just enough so that he'd leave her alone and not enough to lure him on.

"Because I like you too much."

His hands dropped from her arms, leaving them unaccountably bereft. "You *like* me too much! What the hell kind of an answer is that?"

She took refuge in a reciprocal anger. "It's the truth, dammit! I'm being as honest as I know how to be, and if your fragile ego can't take it, then you can just get out!"

"To hell with my fragile ego. I want to know what you're raving about! If you *like* me so much—" the word reeked of sarcasm—"then why the brush-off? And don't give me any sanctimonious claptrap about it being for my own good!"

She was trembling with fury. Her bare toes were curled into the worn carpet as she glared up at him, and she snarled, "Don't worry. It's my good I'm considering, not yours. I stand on my own two feet, Roane. If I want to move to South Carolina, I'll damned well move, and if I want to—"

"Hang on there. What does South Carolina have to do with anything?" He sounded truly mystified, and some of the stiffness drained from her rigid back.

"I just meant," she elaborated patiently, "that I'm my own boss. I run my life to suit me, and I intend to go on running it that way. I'm dependent on no one. No one's dependent on me. Furthermore, that's the way it's going to continue." She planted her hands on her hips and waited for his rebuttal.

The scorn he poured over her so scathingly left her cringing in her tracks as he turned away from her. He didn't say a word. He didn't have to.

"Roane," she began tentatively.

"Forget it. You're a good lay, honey, but you're not the only one around." He was being deliberately crude in an effort to hurt her. She knew it, just as she knew she had finally ruined any chance she'd had to win his love.

A chance to win his love! The words echoed hollowly in her head along with the slamming of the door. Was that what this was all about? Oh, good Lord, where was that much-vaunted self-honesty of hers? Was all that business about independence just one more move in the age-old game he had teased her about? Was she unconsciously flinging out reckless challenges in the hopes that he'd pick up the gauntlet?

Cleo dropped down onto the sofa, instinctively choosing the end where Roane had sat, as if the faint remaining trace of his body heat could bond him to her. As she stared wide-eyed at the door that had slammed shut, the tears ran down her face unchecked. How long had she been kidding herself? Since the night he had showed her the playa lakes in the moonlight? Since that ghastly, funny dinner up on the hill?

She didn't believe in love at first sight. She wasn't sure she believed in love at all after the few examples she'd been exposed to so far. It had taken years, but she'd managed to convince herself that the thing called love was merely a brief hallucination that furthered the proliferation of the human species—or at best, a socially acceptable rationalization for lust.

Jutting her trembling chin out, she told herself she hated Roane for tearing down all her neat theories and exposing her to something she wasn't equipped to handle.

If only she didn't *like* him so much! If only she didn't crave him. If only they hadn't made love and traded terrible puns and warmed away the coldness of that bleak old barn on the hill with shared laughter.

The door opened before she could compose herself, and she jumped up, swiping a fist across her drenched eyes. "Roane, I'm—"

Wint stepped inside, his navy blue hair standing proudly on end. "Well, if this don't beat all. I disremember the last time a body set up and waited for me to come home, girl, but you didn't have to worry none. I ain't tetched a drop since sundown."

If only there had been a decent way for her to skip Thanksgiving altogether, Cleo would have snatched at it. At nine-twenty the following morning, she was still in her pajamas, picking fretfully at the design she had cast on her loom. Nollie stopped by, nearly unrecognizable in a shiny serge suit of a lamentable purplish hue.

"The boy cleaned up real good, Miss Cleo. Ever'thing's all ready for you to go to cookin'. I shore do appreciate your takin' over for me so's Wint and me could go visit—ah—hmmmm—a friend."

She made it to the kitchen just before ten. If she'd anticipated an embarrassing moment or two with Roane, she needn't have worried. He was as congenial as anyone could have asked—and as impersonal.

They didn't eat until after two, and this time she insisted on cleaning up the kitchen, if only as an excuse to avoid the company of the others. After that, it was easy enough to explain having to get home to fix something for Wint's supper, and she escaped with nothing more wounding than a blistering look from Roane as he followed her to the door.

"I'll see you in the morning," he told her.

"I'll be busy in the morning."

"We'll be by to collect you to go riding about eight."

Danni called out from the living room to correct him. "Eight! I wouldn't get up at eight for a fire sale at Tiffany's! We'll see you at ten, Cleo!"

The smile still lingered on Cleo's face as she headed her car toward the trailer. She wasn't sure who had come out of that round the winner, but at least she was still on her feet. As for the next day, she'd make a point of going in to Guymon bright and early. It wasn't too soon to be thinking about picking up a few souvenirs to take back home with her. Not that she needed another souvenir. She'd remember this trip for the rest of her life.

At nine the following morning, she was just bracing herself to climb out of bed when Roane's voice reached her through the bedroom door. After the baritone rumble came Wint's cackle, and after that came the sight of Roane's powerful frame filling the opening of her doorway.

"You can't come in here!"

"Is that another challenge?" Roane smiled at her as if they were on the best of terms. "Honey, you ought to know better by now." With that uncanny grace of his, he moved the few feet to sit on the edge of her bed, and when she jerked the quilt over her shoulders, his smile broadened into a grin.

"You're early!"

He shook his head. "I'm late."

"You said ten o'clock," she accused.

"I said eight. Where were you planning to run off to? Don't tell me you were going to be waiting patiently on the doorstep."

Her lips quivered, and she schooled them into a thin line. He knew her too well. "If you'll give me ten minutes, I'll be ready," she said meekly. He'd expected resistance; she'd see how he handled docility.

Except for a slight narrowing of the eyes, he seemed to accept it at face value. "Fine. Ten minutes it is. The others ought to be along by then."

Call it a draw. In just under twelve minutes, she was washed and brushed and hastily crammed into jeans, boots and a Ragg sweater. She reached for a grapefruit on the way out and then changed her mind and made it an apple. If Roane wanted to play a game of nerves, she could take it. With only four more days before she had to start back, it was time to put the whole situation between them into perspective. A shipboard romance—a holiday fling. That was all it was, all it could possibly be.

The air was exhilarating in spite of a threatening bank of dark clouds piling up on the horizon. Danni, resplendent in white jeans and jacket with acres of fringe and a dash of sequins, was in high spirits as she curvetted around Roane on a snowy mare. She was an excellent rider and had been given a horse befitting her skills. Marsha, in a stunning wine-colored leather suit and matching Stetson, seemed equally at home on the back of her more conservative mount.

"I wasn't sure how much riding you'd done, so I played it safe," Roane told her. On the big ugly bay, he had dropped back beside her while Hal and the two other women rode on ahead. "Her name's Kitty."

"Thanks, she's just my speed. Kitty and I will get along fine if you want to go ahead with the others. Danni's marvelous, isn't she?"

Roane didn't even bother to look at the tiny redhead who was racing headlong for the fence instead of the open gate. "Yeah. So you like horses. What else do you do besides weaving and cooking and riding?"

"I work." She shot him a teasing grin just as a shaft of sunlight slanted through a break in the clouds. "The last time I went riding was over five years ago, and I'm usually too tired to do any cooking except on weekends, and as for weaving, I've been working on one set of placemats for over a year." She cocked her head at him. "What is this, get-acquainted hour?"

Roane lifted one wicked eyebrow, and Cleo grimaced at the opening she had given him, but before he could take advantage of it, Danni trotted up to demand her share of his attention. Since Danni considered her share to be one hundred percent, Cleo was left to poke along at her own pace as she gradually accustomed herself to the feel of the saddle again. So far, she was enjoying it, but she had an idea she'd pay later for every minute of pleasure now.

Ahead of her, Marsha and Hal seemed content to amble along at an easy rate. Marsha's laughter rang out frequently, drawing a frown from Danni. Cleo was amused as she watched the younger woman try to juggle the two men. It was obvious that Roane wasn't exactly hanging on to every word Danni was saying. Or even every other word. The very set of his back looked impatient, and his mount snorted expressively when Danni leaned over to grab his arm.

Whatever it was that Roane said next, it was evidently the wrong thing. Danni flung her head back to set her copper-colored curls dancing in the wind, and with a vicious jerk of the reins, she steered her horse off to one side and galloped over to edge between Hal and Marsha.

A hawk soared overhead, and Cleo was reminded of the last time she had been out in that particular section with Roane. She followed the graceful flight until the predator plunged out of sight behind a hill, and then she sighed for no good reason at all.

Just before it started to drizzle, Danni succeeded in prying Hal away from Marsha, and the pair of them cut across toward the stables. Marsha reined in and waited for Roane, and then the two of them waited for Cleo to catch up.

"I think I'll follow their lead," Cleo called out. The rain didn't bother her half as much as did the sight of the couple who waited for her, side by side on their impatient mounts. There was something disturbingly similar in their bearing—as if they were two people capable of taking precisely what they wanted from life.

"You should have worn something waterproof," Marsha remarked, her cool glance raking Cleo's worn jeans and ancient sweater disparagingly.

"I should have stopped for breakfast," Cleo corrected. "Not much body heat in an apple." Not waiting for a reply, she angled along the path Hal and Danni had followed. It would take her close to the ravine, unfortunately, and she'd just as soon not have any more reminders of that particular episode, but with the drizzle beginning to soak through her jeans, she really was getting chilly.

"Wait—we'll come with you," Roane called after her.

Marsha's voice chimed in with something that was lost to Cleo's ears as she prodded her little chestnut mare into a brisker pace.

She had crossed two long, low rises and was headed down the steep incline into the ravine when she first noticed Kitty's uneven gait. "Oh, Lordy, sweetheart, don't let me down now," she muttered. She cast a measuring eye toward the tops of the buildings in the distance. It was no good. Even to her inexperienced eyes, it was obvious that the mare was having difficulty.

Seeking the skimpy shelter of an outcropping of rock, Cleo slid down off the saddle and hastily grabbed the stirrup until she regained her balance. "Tell me where it hurts, girl—not that I can do much about it."

She was still wondering whether or not it was safe to walk a lame horse when Roane appeared above her. He was alone, Marsha having evidently gone on ahead.

The sight of him topping the rise was entirely too reminiscent of that other time, and Cleo felt an unwilling shaft of warm, sweet expectancy streak through her. He sat a horse like a centaur. Watching the easy way he responded to the changing pitch as the big bay picked his way down the steep slope, she found herself itching to slide her hands under the sheepskin jacket and hold onto that lean, hard body.

"Out of gas?" he called laconically, swinging down from the saddle with practiced ease.

"No, my horse broke down. Is there a parts place open, do you suppose?"

Running a hand over the flank of the patient mare, Roane grinned down at her, his expression largely hidden under the sheltering brim of his hat. "Must have picked up a stone."

"Oh, a horse with prehensile hooves," Cleo quipped with brittle nerves. "Maybe she just broke a fingernail."

"Or maybe she just got tired of listening to wisecracks from a fresh easterner." He lifted the right foreleg and then took a pen-knife from his pocket. "Mmmmm . . . that should do it, old girl."

"You mean she's cured, just like that?" Cleo made a reluctant move to remount, and Roane shook his head.

"Better give her a break. Sidewinder here can carry us both—he's done it before, remember?"

She remembered all too well. Avoiding Roane's knowing look, she allowed herself to be swung aboard, squirming to achieve the most comfortable position possible under the circumstances. "Want me to take her reins?"

"She'll follow us. Kitty's smart enough to get in out of the rain."

Cleo didn't try to talk. The rain had set in with a vengeance by then, and the only thing that made it at all bearable was the feel of Roane's solid warmth against her shivering body. She rested her cheek against him and inhaled the sweet muskiness that clung to his jacket. It was almost worth getting drenched.

Rado was unsaddling Marsha's horse. He lifted a hand in greeting as Sidewinder splashed through the mud to the shelter of the shed roof.

Roane said, "Run on up to the house and get warm, honey. I'll be along in a few minutes."

"I'll wait. If you don't mind running me back, I'd like to get out of these wet clothes." Wint's trailer would be a lot warmer and more inviting than anything Roane had to offer, Cleo decided reluctantly as she watched him unsaddle the bay. Below the sheepskin jacket, the wet fabric of his jeans delineated his powerful thighs and long, cleanly muscled calves.

By the time they reached the trailer, the rain was drumming deafeningly on the roof of the car. Wint's truck was missing. He must have gone back to the Widow Potts' for turkey hash. Reluctantly, Cleo reached for the door.

"I'd better come inside with you and check the gas heater. Wint usually turns it off when he leaves," Roane muttered.

Before she could tell him that she was perfectly capable of dealing with a gas heater, he was outside, dodging around the hood of the car to open her door. "Roane, you're crazy," Cleo yelled over the sound of pelting rain on metal.

He pushed in behind her and slammed the door closed, laughing as he slung water from the brim of his hat. "Sorry about that, honey. Could I borrow a towel from you?"

The surface wetness dealt with, he tackled the heater. Then he turned to her, his crooked grin showing off the chipped tooth as he said, "All I need now is a stiff drink, and I might start to thaw out."

Which was precisely what Cleo was afraid of. The ride home, the cozy confinement of his car in all that rain and now the fact that they were alone in the trailer with no one likely to come looking for them had combined to thaw her out far faster than she considered safe.

"A little of your Eau de Vie de Poire would slide down nicely about now," she acknowledged, with some intention of encouraging him to return to his house guests.

He warmed his hands at the heater. "Barring that, a little of your mincemeat pie."

"Sorry—fresh out." She stood her ground, arms crossed on her chest and her chin ready to thrust defensively at the first sign of danger.

Roane swayed easily on his heels, his sooty hair still showing the marks of his hatband. Without speaking a word, without even trying, he was working his spell on her. He met her eyes and held them, and there was nothing to say, nowhere to hide.

"Cleo." He reached for her, and she was in his arms with no awareness of having moved. Her chin fell as her hastily constructed defense crumbled.

"You're all wet," he whispered hoarsely against her hair. His arms were wrapped completely around her, his hands clasping her shoulders as he brushed his face against her damp fringe.

"So are you." Her hands found their way under the bottom of his jacket, and she worked her arms around him, savoring the warmth of him. Her face felt as if it were on fire as the efficient heater swiftly overcame the damp cold. "I'm wind burned." She laughed shakily.

"Udder balm," Roane rasped into her ear. "Made for sore teats—best thing in the world for chapped hands. Couple of pounds left over from our cow-calf days." He was working her pullover sweater up over her ribs.

She wriggled. "It's my face, not my— Watch out. I'm ticklish!"

His hands closed carefully around her rib cage and he held her away to look down into her face. "I know," he murmured. "I remember."

There was an odd look of strain about his face, a harshness that almost resembled pain. Cleo began to shake her head. "No," she whispered. "No, please, Roane," but already her fingers were busy at the horn buttons on his coat and the smaller ones of his chamois shirt. She paused while he tugged her sweater over her head, and then they both began to laugh as, one after another, rain-dampened garments found their way to the floor of the steamy little trailer. It became a contest between them to see who could undress the other one faster, and as arms tangled with legs and feet got caught up in pants legs, they collapsed on the sofa, weak with laughter. By the time Roane had been stripped of everything, Cleo still retained her bra and one sock.

"The win-nah," she crowed triumphantly, waving a forefinger in the air. Her leg was sprawled across Roane's lap where he had been trying to peel off her last sock.

"Have you any idea"—he panted laughingly—"how utterly debauched you look right now?"

"Look who's talking!" She grinned at him, and then they slowly sobered as their eyes caught and held again. Within seconds, the tension flared between them. Roane's features took on that strained look again, the planes of his face flattening out as his eyes darkened. He made no move to disguise what was happening to him, and Cleo's gaze clung desperately to his eyes, his mouth and the pulse that shuddered rapidly at the base of his throat.

"This time you're the one who's overdressed for the occasion," he told her softly. Stroking the calf of her leg, he slipped his fingers under her sock and shucked it from her foot, and his fingers lingered to caress the high, narrow arch before beginning the return journey.

Cleo's lips parted on a tremulous sigh as his fingers blazed a lingering trail up the inside of her thigh. Her head fell back, and her eyes closed, and when his hand closed tenderly over the seal of her femininity, she whimpered with need. Fragments of warning flickered in her mind like snowflakes, only to melt in the blinding, white-hot fire that threatened to consume her.

"Kiss me—please," Roane commanded, his voice a rasping sound at the back of his throat.

Cleo took his face in her hands and gazed into the smoldering depths of his eyes. Then she lowered her parted lips to each eyelid, in turn, and then to his nose—that crooked, aggressive, masculine blade. She kissed his chin, drawing her tongue lingeringly along the angle of his jaw, and then she buried her face in his neck, nibbling her way down the most sensitive trail to the hollow at the base of his throat.

He shuddered as she scoured each curve of his collarbone with her tongue, and when she brushed her bared teeth over the dark red nailheads embedded in the luxuriant pelt on his chest, he groaned aloud.

She sank her teeth gently into the hard flesh of his abdomen, shuddering against the temptation to bite harder. She wanted to absorb him into her very consciousness, to feel what he felt when she kissed him there... and there.

"Oh, great God, sweetheart, what are you doing to me?" He moaned, lifting her so that she lay across his panting body. "I'm only human."

"I noticed that," she murmured, heady with a feeling of unaccustomed power.

"Not here," Roane muttered rawly, gathering her into his arms to stride toward her bedroom. He shouldered open the door, lowering her onto the bed, and then he followed her down. "You're not still cold?"

"No—are you?"

He laughed shakily. "Are you crazy?" And then his mouth came down on hers, and he raked his hands down her sides until they fanned out over the swell of her hips. "Cleo, Cleo, Cleo, the taste of you is like nectar," he whispered against her lips.

A fleeting thought ran through her mind—alfalfa blossoms—and then it was lost as she felt his hands begin a slow, incendiary journey of exploration. Fondling the soft slopes of her breasts, he lowered his head to scour one nipple with his hot tongue, and a stifled sound escaped her. Her thighs quivered with the need to cradle his taut hips.

"Not yet." He demurred at her small instinctive movements. "You drove me quietly out of my head in there, and now it's your turn." Matching his actions to his words, he proceeded to sample every part of her body, leaving kisses in each small hollow, along the crest of every curve. Her eyes widened as molten lava began to course through the valley of her desire, and she pleaded with him to end the sweet torture in the only way possible.

Instead, he rolled over onto his back and turned his head to face her. The black-gold gleam of his eyes was shuttered under heavy eyelids as he said, "Give me your hand."

One by one, he kissed each of her fingers. Nibbling at the sensitive pad at the base of her thumb, he watched her, savoring the raw hunger he saw on her face. God, if he could just make it last forever. She was overflowing with passion, so ripe and sweet, and he wanted her more than he'd ever wanted anything in his life. He wanted everything she had to offer—and not just for tonight.

Her hand escaped his, and her fingers tangled in the hair on his chest. At her touch on his flat nipples, his hips thrust sharply, and the muscles of his abdomen were racked with tremors. Damn—he had no more control than a first-time kid! Taking a deep, shuddering breath, he willed himself to slow down.

"You're ticklish, too," Cleo crowed in soft triumph, some of the playfulness returning to her now that the white-hot heat had abated momentarily. Then her hands were all over him again, making daring little forays to circle his navel, to trace the small scar on his groin he'd got when he was eight and had tried to ride a Brahma bull. "How did you get this scar?"

Her hands were driving him wild—cupping, cradling, stroking with an unselfconscious touch that almost sent him over the edge. "A riding accident." He grunted. "Honey—you're killing me by sweet degrees—come here."

He raised her, settling her down on him with exquisite slowness so that her long, satiny legs were curled at his sides. His hands lifted to stroke her shoulders, and then he brought her down until her breasts swung like small, tantalizing pears just above his hungry mouth.

Desperately he tried to hold back, but by now the momentum was too great. As her movements became more and more frenzied, he began to thrust powerfully with his hips, and then, in his last lucid moment before the world exploded, he heard a sweet flurry of descending notes cascade over him to end on a whispered sigh.

Ten

Cleo opened her eyes. Roane was breathing quietly beside her now. They had both slept, safely cocooned by the rain as they drifted in that mindless state of delicious afterglow.

But the rain had stopped, and the morning had melted into afternoon, and any minute now they were apt to be interrupted by Wint, or by someone from up on the hill, demanding attention.

"Are you awake?" she asked softly. If only this moment didn't have to end, she thought. If only she dared follow her emotions and instincts one step further.

Roane had been awake all along. Having managed with remarkable difficulty to shelve his own emotions, he began to apply reason to the problem at hand. All it would take was one misstep and she'd scurry back into that shell of hers, and he'd never pry her out. Her vacation was almost over. A week, a few days at most, and she'd leave, and he'd never see her again.

He didn't think he could stand it. He'd never even realized how meaningless his life had become until she'd showed up. Call it chemistry, call it what you will—all he knew was that he had to have her, had to keep her in his life, and if she laughed at him this time, he didn't think he could bear it.

He brought a phrase to the tip of his tongue, and it tasted false. The last time he'd spouted any palaver about love, he hadn't known the meaning of the word, and now, when he felt it so damn deeply that it almost tore him apart, he couldn't bring himself to speak.

"I think the sun's trying to come out," Cleo murmured.

He stirred, and the arm he had flung across her tightened instinctively. He made himself release her. *Easy now,* he cautioned. *Take it one step at a time. Don't rush your fences.*

Her own arms closed over her body where his had been. "Wint should be back before too long, don't you think? He didn't mention where he was going this morning, did he?" Her voice held a curiously brittle note.

Roane mumbled something vaguely placating. He was too busy trying to weigh the tone of her voice to be concerned with her words. She couldn't actually be worried about the old man at a time like this—she was just making space for herself. He'd noticed this way she had of backing off when things got too tense.

On the other hand, she also had a well-developed sense of duty. How many women would drive this far just to visit a cantankerous old relative whose only assets were a mangy goat and half a dozen roosters? Certainly not any of the avaricious females he knew.

There had to be a way of making that overgrown sense of duty work for him. All he had to do was to keep her here long enough to talk her into taking him seriously. He'd cried wolf once too often, damn it, and she thought he was still joking.

Maybe he had been at first. The old man had started it, and he'd enjoyed teasing her about it, but now, all of a sudden, the joke was on him. Nothing else mattered except keeping her here where he could gradually win her confidence and then try to win her love. The thought of having her laugh in his face again twisted his gut until he could hardly stand it!

Feigning a casualness he was far from feeling, he said, "I reckon folks up at the house will be getting hungry pretty soon now. Think you could rustle up enough of that turkey for a few sandwiches?"

Cleo continued to stare up at the pink plastic ceiling fixture. Slowly, it blurred before her eyes, and she blinked quickly. "I'll put together something," she said in a commendably casual voice. "You'd better go on up to the house and tell them help is on the way."

Hal and Danni left just before dark. Hal claimed the pressure of business, and Danni, openly staking her claim, flung a triumphant look at Marsha and followed him out to his car. That left Marsha, Roane and Cleo.

When Cleo made her own excuses to leave, Roane's hands were tied. Marsha had just brought down several books of house plans that she just "happened to have with her," and he looked helplessly from one woman to the other. Cleo didn't give him a chance to extricate himself even if he'd wanted to. With a brilliant smile and a word about fixing Wint's supper, she let herself out the front door.

Roane was three steps behind her, a look of dark thunder on his face. "Hey! What about those window shades? Weren't we going to hang the things tonight?"

Cleo smiled a guileless smile that didn't quite reach her eyes. "Oh, were we? I didn't think it mattered, now that most of your guests have left. Marsha will help you—it's her line, not mine."

"Damn it, wait a minute!"

Sliding under the wheel, Cleo gunned the engine ruthlessly, casting up a spray of gravel as she backed recklessly around and headed out the driveway toward the trailer. Halfway there, the tears threatened to blind her, and she was forced to pull over and blow her nose.

How could he be so insensitive? So unfeeling? To make love to her, to disarm her so completely and then ask her to go feed his girlfriends, to hang his blasted window shades while he drooled over house plans with that—that—*decorator!* It was Doug Parkins all over again; only this time, instead of twenty-one long-stemmed roses and the tag end of a subscription to Forbes, all she'd got was a bowl of cactus and a battered ego.

Wint was still out, and she couldn't wait another minute. She simply had to put the dust of Oklahoma behind her before she made an even bigger fool of herself. He still hadn't come home by the time she had thrown everything she could find into her suitcase, and she scribbled a note and left it on the kitchen counter. Maybe Wint would believe she wanted to see the alabaster caves and the salt plains enough to leave early, and maybe he wouldn't. She'd call him that night and make some excuse, but for now, she couldn't face his well-meaning inquisition. He was too shrewd not to guess what was wrong with her and too conniving not to try and do something about it.

In Guymon, she tried to call from a gas station, but there was no answer. Her conscience was already bothering her for running out, and she rationalized furiously as she headed southeast on 270.

She'd had no choice. How could any man be so monstrously unfeeling after what had just happened between them? It wasn't as if she'd made any emotional demands on him. It had been a mutual thing, their coming together—both times it had been as much her fault as his, but she hadn't asked him for any commitment. She hadn't asked him for anything, but dear God, did he have to be so callous about it? Couldn't he at least have pretended? If just once he'd told her he loved her, whether or not he really did, she might have salvaged her pride. As it was, there was nothing left to salvage.

It was almost nine when she pulled into Woodward. The first motel she saw looked adequate, and she didn't look any further. First she'd call Wint, then she'd grab a bite to eat, and then she'd set about forgetting everything connected with Roane Gallagher and his damned ranch!

This time, Wint answered on the second ring. It took all the considerable skills at her command to explain why she had found it necessary to rush off without waiting to say good-bye, and she wasn't at all certain she had succeeded. "Look, Wint, I'd have had to leave in a couple of days, anyway. I thought I'd look at the caves, spend a day hunting for crystals on the salt plains and maybe look up a museum that has a collection of Indian weaving."

"Roane didn't have nothing to do with this, did he?" the old man asked suspiciously.

"Roane! Why should you think that? We certainly didn't quarrel, if that's what you mean. Look, Wint, I'm starved, and this place looks like it might shut down early. I'll call when I get home, and—and I love you. Bye!"

There—it was done. Staring blindly at the woodgrained plastic of the motel table, she decided she'd leave at four in the morning and try to make it home in two days instead of three. Before going out in search of something to eat, she left a call for three-forty-five.

When the rattling noise woke her up, she'd been sleeping heavily and dreamlessly. She blinked her eyes open and waited, and when it came again, she slapped clumsily at the phone. The mechanical hum that greeted her instead of the cheery good morning she'd expected left her more confused than ever.

It was the door. Her wake-up call? With some hazy notion about the night clerk's not ringing the rooms in the middle of the night to keep from disturbing the other guests, she felt her way sleepily to the door. She flipped the latch, left the chain intact and exposed her nose, chin and eyelids to a crack of frosty morning air.

"G'morning. Thanks, I'm up," she mumbled, slurring her words together.

"Cleo!"

The eyelids popped open, and she blinked away the fogginess. "Roane?"

"Let me in."

"Go away!" She was hallucinating. The man leaning on her door frame, sheepskin collar turned up around his green face, couldn't be—his green face? "Roane?" she repeated uncertainly.

"Please, Cleo, let me inside before I embarrass myself."

Fumbling with the chain, she threw open the door, her concerned gaze following Roane's lurching progress toward the bed. He flopped backward, sliding his Stetson over his face.

"Give me a minute—five minutes," he mumbled.

For three of the five, Cleo stood by the door, staring at the man who sprawled, hatted, coated and booted, across her bed. And then, her heart racing at a dizzying speed, she tiptoed around to the other side and cautiously lifted his hat from his face. It must have been a trick of the light that had made him look so ghastly—he couldn't have been that green. On the other hand, he was still awfully pale. Something was wrong. Something was definitely wrong here.

"Roane, what's happened? How did you find me? What are you doing here? Has something happened to Wint?"

Reluctantly, he opened one eye. "Look, we're not going through that routine again, are we? Wint's fine. Sends his regards." He groaned and raked his fingers through his hair. "You wouldn't have any brandy on you, would you?"

Dropping to the bed, Cleo curled a leg beneath her and shook her head. "Would you mind telling me what's going on? How did you—"

"He found your note when he got home and called up to the house. Seemed to think I might have some idea why you'd vamoosed. After that, there was nothing to do but wait for you to call again. You mentioned the caves and the salt plains, and we couldn't be sure where you'd hole up for the night."

"I decided to push on through," Cleo murmured almost apologetically.

"But why? Cleo, what the devil got into you to make you jump and run that way?" He sounded genuinely puzzled, and she gazed down at him ruefully, taking in the pallor and the harried expression.

If she'd had any doubts about her feelings, they'd been settled once and for all by one look at that pale, miserable face. He looked perfectly terrible, and she'd never loved anyone so much in her life as she did this big, untidy man who was sprawled across her bed. "I just thought it might be better all around," she ventured.

"Better! What the devil's better about worrying everybody to death? What was so all fired important that it couldn't wait another day?" He rolled over and sat up to glare at her, and the bedside lamp highlighted the film of perspiration on his high, unnaturally pale forehead.

"Roane, are you feeling all right?"

"No, I'm not feeling all right! I'm sick as a dog and mad as hell, and if I don't get a few straight answers pretty damned fast, you're going to be feeling even worse than I am!"

The more he railed at her, the more distraught Cleo became. She jumped up and rummaged in her suitcase for something to pull on over her pajamas. The brown cardigan was the first thing that came to hand, and she slung it over her shoulders. Before she could return to the bed, Roane had hauled himself up and headed for the bathroom, tossing his coat to the floor. When he emerged again his hair and the collar of his shirt were wet, but at least some of his normal color seemed to have returned.

"Would you mind telling me what's wrong with you?" she demanded. She sniffed suspiciously, but all she could smell was the familiar muskiness of the sheepskin coat and Roane's own clean, healthy scent. "Are you drunk or just hung over?"

"In a word," he said succinctly, "I'm airsick."

"Oh, no—Roane, I'm so sorry. Maybe you'd better lie down again."

He took the chair, looking somewhat mollified and considerably healthier than he had a few minutes before. "I'll be all right. Next time, though, I'd appreciate it if you'd give me more notice. As it was, I couldn't move until I got the word from Wint about where you'd called from, and then I had to make tracks in a hurry to haul Marsha to Oklahoma City and double back before you'd jumped the gun on us again."

"But why? I mean, why did you come after me, and why take Marsha home—and why couldn't Pete have done it for you?" At his grimace that passed for a smile, something twisted inside her. It was all she could do not to gather him in her arms and croon to him.

"In the first place," he said dryly, "Marsha was in the way. She knew what was going on, and she was as ready to leave as I was to get rid of her. As for Pete—somehow I couldn't see him barging into your room in the middle of the night to tell you how much his boss loved you and wanted you to come back. There are some jobs a man likes to do for himself."

Careful, Cleo warned herself breathlessly. *You could wake up any minute now and it would all be gone.* Poof! No Roane, no battered Stetson hanging on the doorknob, no honey-colored eyes reaching inside her to tear the very heart from her. "Roane, are you trying to tell me that you came after me because you *love* me?"

He stood up and rammed his hands in his pockets, shoving the jeans that clung to his narrow hips dangerously low. "What the devil have I been saying all this time?" he growled, shrugging his massive shoulders. "Why else would I subject myself to all this agony if it weren't important? You're damned right I love you, and before you start laughing, let me tell you something else—I'm not at all sure you don't love me, too! A woman doesn't make love to a man and then skip out the way you did unless she's running scared. You aren't afraid of *me,* so it has to be *you,* and when I ask myself what you're afraid of, I come up with some pretty intriguing answers."

Her sound of dismay went unnoticed as he continued to stalk the small room like a caged hawk. "Don't argue. Just try to sit back and listen to me for two minutes without making any smart cracks, if you can manage it."

"I wasn't—"

"There you go again. Cleo, I've had the devil of a time working up my nerve, and I rehearsed this all the way from the airport, so don't interrupt me or I'll lose my place. Now—where was I?"

"Airport?" she prompted helpfully.

He glared at her. "No, damn it, I was about to propose to you again, so will you pipe down? In the first place, I don't know a whole lot about the so-called tender emotions. I don't remember my mother, and my dad would have cut out his tongue before he spoke a kind word. Oh, he was a good man—none better—only as far as he was concerned, softness equated with weakness, and he despised weakness."

Cleo's eyes followed him as some of the fierce tension seemed to leave his broad back, seeing glimpses of the child and the rebellious boy in the man who confronted her now.

"All I know about love I learned from those two old men back at the ranch," Roane went on, pacing a tight pattern on the floor. "We don't talk about it, but Nollie's always been there when I needed him. He and Wint were the two things in my life that I could count on. If I got drunk and raised hell, they dried me out or bailed me out—or both. And they didn't think any the less of me for it. I haven't needed much in the way of wet nursing these past twenty years or so, but if I did, they'd be still there for me."

He turned to her then, a silent plea in his eyes, and Cleo stood up and crossed swiftly to wrap her arms around his middle. "I know, darling. I know," she murmured soothingly.

His hand came up to cup the back of her neck, and he pressed her face against his chest. "Maybe I should have taken some courting lessons from them while I was at it. As a lover, I sure as hell don't win any awards, but Cleo—sweetheart—" With his thumb, he tilted her face so that he could gaze down at her. "I do love you. It just felt so—so natural, so right, that it took me a while to figure out what was going on. I've never even come close to feeling this—this wholeness before. So if you want to laugh, then go ahead, but if you want to leave me . . . well, I'm not sure I can let you go."

She dug her face into his throat, laughter edging dangerously close to tears as she said, "Leave you! Oh, Roane, you'll never get rid of me now. I guess I just panicked. I was afraid of repeating an old pattern and winding up the loser again."

"Would this pattern have anything to do with the reason you were so skittish? I mean, outside of a couple of notable exceptions"—he grinned provocatively—"I reckon what happened between us on a physical level was pure spontaneous combustion, but every time I tried to get inside your head, you shut me out.''

Her hands slipped up under his arms and curled into the resilient muscles as she sorted through the words to explain Doug and how his defection had affected her. ''I just didn't want to be used again; that's all.'' She sighed. ''I'm not a—a household appliance, to be taken out and used as long as a man needs me and then crammed back in the closet and forgotten.''

Roane stroked her back with a soothing touch. ''Oh, sweetheart,'' he whispered brokenly, ''you underestimate yourself if you think I could ever *ever* forget you. It was too late for me after that first day—only I didn't have the sense to know what had happened to me.''

He kissed her eyes, her cheeks, the tip of her nose, and last of all, her mouth. She was still hungry for him when he lifted his face to say, ''Maybe we both had to go through some pain to get to the place where we were ready for each other. Philosophy's not my long suit, but I'll lay odds we'd have gotten together somehow, somewhere, if I'd had to walk to North Carolina and trip over my feet on your doorstep.''

Philosophy was the least of her worries now. Centered in the warmth that encompassed her was that small, volatile spark that could so swiftly flare up to burn out of control. With one last effort to be rational, she said, "There's my job."

"Forget it. If you have any energy left over after running me and my outfit, I'll help you find some way to work it off." He began edging them toward the bed.

"I don't know—maybe I'll be too exhausted. It's a big spread, and I have all sorts of ideas about making it more comfortable." Her fingers were working diligently on the buttons of his shirt, and she slid her hands inside.

Nor was Roane exactly idle. Her cardigan fell unnoticed to the floor, and her pajama top soon followed. "Honey, if you want to demolish that old barn on the hill, I'll build you anything you want—for a wedding present." One of his hands was sensuously massaging her waistline, dipping into the shallow valley of her spine and returning to the small cup of her navel.

When the hand slipped down under her waistband, Cleo found it almost impossible to speak. "Don't touch a hair on the head of that old barn," she gasped. "It's an honest house, and I like an honest house that doesn't pretend to be anything but what it is.''

His mouth against her throat, Roane murmured, ''That's one way of looking at it.''

Cleo leaned back to scowl at him, and he compounded the effect of her movement by pulling her hips even closer to his. ''Well— maybe a new heating system,'' she conceded weakly.

''And a king-size bed, and a bathtub for two—the necessities of life.'' Roane's fingers tangled with hers as she fumbled frantically with his silver buckle.

''For someone who was wobbling around on his last legs a few minutes ago, you seem to have staged a remarkable recovery,'' Cleo jeered as she dealt efficiently with a short zipper. The race was on again, and this time she was going to lose—Roane had on too many clothes. She shoved him down on the bed and grabbed a boot.

''A little physical therapy will do wonders,'' he said modestly, as he helped her with the task at hand. When they were both undressed, he pulled her to him, and they sprawled, laughing, across the bed. ''But just to be on the safe side, we'd better have a dose of honey, too.''

She met his lips eagerly, savoring the lovely knowledge that he was all hers. ''The sweetest kind of honey,'' she murmured into his lips.

* * * * *

Harlequin Romance ®

Delightful

Affectionate

Romantic

Emotional

Tender

Original

Daring

Riveting

Enchanting

Adventurous

Moving

Harlequin Romance—the
series that has it all!

HROM-G

HARLEQUIN ❖ PRESENTS®

HARLEQUIN PRESENTS
men you won't be able to resist falling in love with...

HARLEQUIN PRESENTS
women who have feelings just like your own...

HARLEQUIN PRESENTS
powerful passion in exotic international settings...

HARLEQUIN PRESENTS
intense, dramatic stories that will keep you turning
to the very last page...

HARLEQUIN PRESENTS
The world's bestselling romance series!

LOOK FOR OUR FOUR FABULOUS MEN!

Each month some of today's bestselling authors bring four new fabulous men to Harlequin American Romance. Whether they're rebel ranchers, millionaire power brokers or sexy single dads, they're all gallant princes—and they're all ready to sweep you into lighthearted fantasies and contemporary fairy tales where anything is possible and where all your dreams come true!

You don't even have to make a wish...Harlequin American Romance will grant your every desire!

Look for Harlequin American Romance wherever Harlequin books are sold!

What do women really want to know?

Trust the world's largest publisher of
women's fiction to tell you.

HARLEQUIN ULTIMATE GUIDES™

I CAN FIX THAT

A Guide For Women
Who Want To Do It Themselves

This is the only guide a self-reliant
woman will ever need to deal
with those pesky items that
break, wear out or just don't work
anymore. Chock-full of friendly
advice and straightforward,
step-by-step solutions to the
trials of everyday life in our
gadget-oriented world! So, don't
just sit there wondering how to
fix the VCR—run to your
nearest bookstore for your copy now!

Available this May, at your favorite retail outlet.

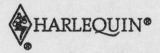

FIX